The ZEE FILES

The ZEE FILES

BY TINA WELLS

with Stephanie Smith
Illustrated by Veronica Miller Jamison

WEST
MARGIN
PRESS

For Phoebe. I hope I've succeeded in creating
characters you will love.

And for my family and friends, without whom
none of this would be possible.

Written with Stephanie Smith
Illustrated by Veronica Miller Jamison
Art Direction by Melissa Alam

ISBN: 9781513266268

Printed in Canada

24 23 22 21 2 3 4 5

Published by West Margin Press

WEST
MARGIN
PRESS

WestMarginPress.com

WEST MARGIN PRESS
Publishing Director: Jennifer Newens
Marketing Manager: Angela Zbornik
Editor: Olivia Ngai
Design & Production: Rachel Lopez Metzger

1

THE "SEE YOU LATER"

"You think they have Umami Burger in London?" Mackenzie Blue Carmichael asked her mother as she surveyed her room. Zee never thought she'd say goodbye to her personal sanctuary/recording studio/research laboratory/ headquarters for all things Zee, but here they were, leaving on a jet plane. To London. In just one week.

"I'm not sure, darling," Mrs. Carmichael replied, handing her phone to Zee.

"*Darling?*" Zee wondered when all of a sudden her mother turned into the Duchess of Cambridge. "Since when do you say 'darling'?"

"Since... oh, don't make fun," said Mrs. Carmichael. "Now, what I do know is that I made a master list of all of the amazing places to eat, drink, and play when we get there."

Zee expected to see the Notes app pulled up on her mom's phone with a list of restaurants, museums, and shops in London. Instead, Mrs. Carmichael had a browser window of Goop.com open to a list written by Gwyneth Paltrow recommending her favorite haunts of the city.

"Is she even British?" Zee asked of the website's founder.

"Does it matter? She's been there a hundred times for movies and photo shoots."

"Ah," Zee replied. "Makes her an expert."

Zee slumped on her bed while her mother rolled in two oversized brightly colored suitcases in an attempt to prod her eldest daughter to start packing.

"London," Zee said with a sigh. "Do they even have palm trees? Does the sun even shine? Why couldn't Dad get a job closer to home?"

"Because this is a *better* job," Mrs. Carmichael said, waving her hand for Zee to give her phone back. Her curly sun-kissed hair was swept back into a high bun and her freckled cheeks were rosy from the effort of packing. "He's the big boss of a

major advertising agency and will be doing most of his work with European companies. Consider it an adventure."

Mrs. Carmichael stacked Zee's suitcases close to her bed while Zee got up and opened the closet door to survey her belongings. Several pairs of Veja sneakers ("They use organic cotton and recycled plastic bottles in their shoes," Zee told her mom when she bought them) customized with rhinestones, patches, and hand-painted designs—all artwork done by Zee herself—lined the bottom of her closet. Her clothes hung snugly on the rack, crammed in after years of collecting old concert T-shirts, vintage dresses, and other costumes for The Beans, the band she was in with her friends, and their gigs in talent shows and local showcases. Bookbags and other totes hung from the side wall on special ceramic hooks Zee designed on a rainy weekend, while caps and other hats perched above the clothes. Stacked on the floor near the shoes sat a number of mismatched boxes filled with years of personal artifacts that Zee now had to open, sort, and repack—or, sigh, throw away—for transport to London.

Stepping out of the closet, Zee looked around her room. The sun shone in through the bay window opposite her four-poster bed, the rays beaming across the window bench and onto her bright-blue bean bag, creating a warm, toasty spot to relax.

Zee's phone buzzed. The screen showed a notification for a message from her Brookdale bestie, Chloe Lawrence-Johnson.

Chloe

> **Still on for tonight?**
> **I'll bring snacks.**

Zee and Chloe were having one last sleepover before she took off for London next weekend. All summer, Chloe and Zee maximized their remaining time together. They had ice cream at Jeni's Ice Cream and tacos at Furious Tacos in Venice. They hung out at The Grove and walked the Venice Boardwalk. They rode bikes and met up to write songs and research celebrity deaths (Chloe wanted to be an editor at *Vanity Fair* when she grew up).

Now, for their last night together, they needed to make a schedule for long-distance phone calls and video sessions so they could stay in touch. It was going to be a long—but fun—night.

• • •

"Ugh. Girl. I mean. Whyyyy... do you have to move so far awayyy?" Chloe asked as she came in the front door of Zee's house wearing a red tracksuit, her hair in two thick French braids that bounced off her back. She took off her custom Stan Smiths in the entryway and gave Zee a hug.

"I knowww!" Zee said. "London is cold. And do they even recycle there?"

"I'm sure they do, they're not savages. England has been around centuries longer than the U.S."

Chloe handed Zee a bag filled with smaller bags that were organized with snacks, crackers, pretzels, popcorn bites, and Zee's favorite cacao nib–covered caramels. "I brought all of your favorite snacks, and some for the plane ride over," Chloe explained.

"Ahh, bestie! That's awesome, thank you!"

The girls walked through the family room, past boxes full of small furniture and appliances that Zee's mom has already packed to ship over to their new English home. They entered the kitchen where Mrs. Carmichael was hovering over Zee's eighteen-month-old twin siblings Phoebe and Connor with her phone in hand. The twins were dressed in matching outfits, a strategy that helped Mrs. Carmichael amass 10,000 followers on her Instagram, @twobycarmichael.

"Seriously, Mom, you are doing so much damage to not only these poor children's egos, but our planet! What's with you buying the twins so many things that they'll only fit into once?"

"It's for the 'gram! Hello, Chloe, my dear. How are you?" Mrs. Carmichael greeted, hugging Zee's friend.

"Hi, Mrs. Carmichael," Chloe replied, then turned to the babies in their twin white linen jumpsuits. "Hi, little friends!"

"I'm sure you must be sad to see Zee leave," Mrs. Carmichael said.

"Of course, but we're going to keep in touch with as many conference calls and text messages as possible. It'll be like she never left!"

Zee grabbed two green juices and some strawberries from the refrigerator and shut the door. She walked by the twins playing with a toy truck between them and kissed their little foreheads before leaving the kitchen with Chloe following behind her. They climbed the stairs to the second floor and headed to Zee's bedroom.

Chloe plopped her bookbag down on Zee's sheepskin floor rug and took out her iPhone, iPad, laptop, and camera, all the devices one needed to manage the activities of a soccer star/ investigative celebrity reporter. Chloe had played with Zee's band The Beans for two years, but her soccer schedule became more demanding ever since she joined a traveling team, the Galaxy. Now she barely had time for school and her Instagram feed.

"Okay, let's make sure we have all of our accounts synced," Chloe said as all screens on the four devices lit up. "Squad?"

"Yes," Zee replied.

"Zoom?"

"Yes."

"WhatsApp?"

"Yep!"

"TikTok?"

"Yes."

"Voxer?"

"Yes."

"Quallmi?"

"Yes."

"TXT?"

"Yes. Wait." Zee retyped the password in her phone. She always forgot the login for TXT. "Yes."

"Mssg?"

"Yes."

"I think we're good!" Chloe declared. "We'll never be out of touch."

"How do you focus with all of those notifications going off all the time?" Zee teased.

"Years of training," Chloe said.

Zee took a seat in the sunny spot on the bean bag and

sighed. "I'm going into an entirely new life in London! New friends. New school. What if I don't like it?"

"Then you'll just come back," Chloe said.

"I can't come back without my mom and dad."

"You can always come and live with me and my parents. They'd love to have you!"

The two munched on strawberries. *Would Chloe and I share a room?* Zee thought.

"Did you say goodbye to Landon?" Chloe asked of Zee's longtime crush and sort-of-boyfriend-not-boyfriend. Zee continued to look down at her popcorn.

"No. Honestly, I don't want to say goodbye to anyone," Zee said defiantly. "Not Landon, not you, not my house. This whole thing for me is just 'see you later.'"

"Yeah," Chloe said. "Much later."

Zee took a few swigs of her green juice and wiped her mouth. She looked around her room, at photos of her Brookdale friends, and finally at Chloe again. She opened the bag of snacks Chloe brought and popped one of the cacao nib caramels in her mouth.

"I'll be back for Christmas," Zee said. "Not that much later."

After pizza with the family, Chloe and Zee changed into their PJs: Chloe in a pink onesie she bought after seeing Yara Shahidi wear the same one on Instagram, and Zee in an old Beans T-shirt and a pair of gym shorts. "Why buy new pajamas for nighttime when you can just recycle clothes you don't wear in the daytime?" Zee said with a shrug. They spent all night choreographing Snapchat and TikTok dance videos, some of which they shared, others they reviewed on their phones and laughed at together. Then they watched old movies—"*Mean Girls* is a classic!" Chloe said—and eventually passed out in front of the TV in the family room.

The next morning Chloe's mom picked her up after breakfast, since Zee had to start packing and run some errands with her mom. Zee offered Chloe a few mementos from her closet she didn't think she'd need in London. "I'll take that denim vest with the peace patch we wore during our '70s-themed Beans performance off your hands," Chloe said. Finally, they said their see-you-laters.

"It will be just like you still live close by," Chloe said.

"Right," Zee said. She waved then closed her front door before her best friend could see tears well up in the corner of her eyes.

2

HELLO, LONDON!

Zee raised her hand to get the attention of the teacher at the front of the room, but she wouldn't call on her. That's rude, *Zee thought. She just wanted her to repeat the homework assignment. Then Zee noticed everyone in the class was staring at her. They started to snicker, then sneer, then shake their heads. Zee looked down, mortified. Somehow, sitting in the middle of the classroom in front of the most attractive eighth graders she'd ever seen (was that Noah Centineo toward the front of the room?), she realized she'd left home wearing just her bra, a pair of striped underpants, and striped socks. Zee's hand shrank from the sky...*

"Darling!" Mrs. Carmichael said, patting Zee awake. "Would you like something to drink?"

Zee shook her head, blinking her eyes, and looked at her mother. She patted herself down and saw that not only did she have on clothes, she was covered up by a blanket and still in her seat on the flight from Los Angeles to London.

"Um, sorry. Yes, water is fine, thanks."

Zee's nightmare rattled her awake long enough to come back to reality. The flight attendant handed Mrs. Carmichael a small cup of water and a napkin, and Mrs. Carmichael passed them on to Zee. Zee looked over her left shoulder through the crack between the plane and her seat and saw her father reclined in his seat in the row behind watching a movie, his headphones cushioning his ears and the headband cutting across his wavy red hair ("a gift from our Irish ancestors," he often proudly said). To Zee's right, the twins were sound asleep in their seats, holding onto one another as if they were still in the womb. Her mother readjusted the blanket covering both of their small bodies.

Zee sipped some water and opened a small bag of mini pretzels as she gazed out the window, longing for other thoughts to calm her anxiety about moving. She thought about her friends at Brookdale Academy. Her BFF Ally Stern was someone she talked to every day until Ally left California to move to Paris with her journalist parents. Ally and Chloe were Zee's closest friends—Zee's known Ally since they were in kindergarten and only met Chloe about a year ago, though they all bonded so easily it seemed like they've been friends since they were little too. Friendships like that don't come around every day.

Then there was Landon Beck, who also went to Brookdale. They were friends, but last year deeper feelings started to run between them. But when Landon attempted to kiss her, things got weird, and Zee realized she didn't want *that* type of relationship with him. The two didn't speak much around the end of last year. Things felt—what did he say in his last note to Zee?—*unfinished* with poor Landon.

One person she was happy to think about was Jasper Chapman. Jasper had moved from London to California at the beginning of sixth grade but then went back to London at the end of seventh grade to be closer to his family. Jasper, a musician and music engineer, produced his own music, and he and Zee grew close over their common interests. Zee's parents found out where Jasper was attending school from his family and enrolled Zee in the same school, just so she would have at least one mate in her new environment. Zee was thrilled to learn she would be going to school with Jasper in London. "When you arrive," he told her, "I'll show you all the really fun, non-touristy spots."

The Carmichaels were just a few hours into their flight to London, but Zee missed her California pals already. She thought wistfully about the way things were: their comfortable school, their tree-lined block in their subdivision, her three-speed bicycle that she rode to school and to the smoothie shop around the corner. Her mind forgot about her nightmare of arriving at school naked as she stared at the clouds outside turning pink as the sun set over the land 36,000 feet below. Zee's eyes grew heavy, then her head drifted over to one side. She fell back asleep, hoping to find happier times of a London future in her dreams.

• • •

"We're home!" Mr. Carmichael announced as they pulled up to a three-story home in Notting Hill, the stylish London neighborhood with classically designed townhomes, sleek

boutiques, and trendy restaurants. Zee was in the back row of an SUV with her mother, her head resting on the window ledge. Zee's stomach rumbled a bit, and she thought about the last non-airplane food meal she ate.

The family spilled out of the car onto the sidewalk and looked up and down their tree-lined street before turning toward their new home. The house looked inviting, with a wrought iron and wood door and tidy shrubs in the windowsills, like a home out of an episode of *Fixer Upper: London Edition*. The stairs leading up to the front door were tucked behind a metal gate and a patch of grass that was only big enough to spread out a picnic blanket. Zee wondered if that was all the green space the house had.

"There's more grass in the garden," Mr. Carmichael said. "C'mon, let's check out your new home."

Mr. Carmichael went ahead to open the front door and waved to the rest of the family to follow him inside. As they did, the moving truck packed with their belongings from the California home pulled up right behind the SUV.

"Oh, how delightful," Mrs. Carmichael said as she walked in slowly, her phone filming in one hand to give her IG followers a first look at the house before the movers and boxes got in the way.

Since Mrs. Carmichael was now a social influencer, she wanted their U.K. home to be well lit and have enviable features, like a palm tree–wallpapered wall, a garden in the back, and a large kitchen with an island. The interior of their home was surprisingly spacious for a London townhouse enhanced by high ceilings and an all-white interior. The living room led into a big kitchen with a skylight, and from there sliding glass doors opened out to the garden, a beautifully groomed space big enough for a small swing set for the twins, a picnic table, and a barbecue.

Upstairs Zee found four bedrooms and three bathrooms. The main bedroom was located over to one side of the home with a bathroom connected to it. Further down the hallway were another two bedrooms with a bathroom in the middle. One would be for the twins, the other for Zee. The third floor included one last bedroom and an office or playroom, depending on what Mrs. Carmichael wanted to do with the space.

Zee strolled into what would be her room, which was considerably smaller than her bedroom in California. She looked at the bare white walls and the wide rectangular window facing out to the neighborhood. The floors were cold. The closet was compact. Then the movers walked in and plopped her blue bean bag chair down on the floor outside the door. Zee dragged it over by the window and sank into it. She took a deep breath as she looked out the window, seeing the sun reflect off her neighbors' homes across the street. Zee smiled as her body melted into the soft chair. Perhaps this unfamiliar setting could feel like home after all.

• • •

"C'mon, Ally, pick up," Zee said, urging the line to connect to her best friend as her parents walked ahead with the twins past some shops.

Ally lived in Paris, having moved there a year prior with her parents who were both journalists, her father a writer for

The Financial Times, her mother a freelance travel and fashion writer. While Ally had always been quiet and kept to herself, Paris had helped widen her perspective on the world. Her text messages and e-mails always mentioned the museums and interesting people she'd seen in Paris so far. She even signed off her messages in French: *Au revoir!*

Zee sighed, exasperated, as she hung up and hurried to catch up to her family. She hadn't spoken to Ally in what seemed like weeks. Back at Brookdale, Ally was the first person Zee told everything to, right before Chloe. First crush on Landon? Ally knew. Zee always showed Ally her most intimate poetry and writing too. In this crazy time of transition from America to the U.K. and whatever her new school will bring, Zee really needed her pals, especially one who had just gone through the same experience of leaving the California coast for Europe.

After a full day of unpacking, the Carmichaels decided to go out and take in the sights and sound of London. Everything moved so quickly and felt tightly packed here, Zee thought as she walked. There were what seemed like thousands of people on the sidewalks, walking, talking, and drinking coffee. The streets were narrow and slick from rain. Zee's sneakers were already damp after just five minutes of a neighborhood stroll.

"Watch out!" Mr. Carmichael said, grabbing Zee just as she was about to cross the street without looking to her right first. A double-decker bus rolled by, nearly flattening Zee in the crosswalk. "Since cars drive on the left here, you really need to be looking to your right first, then left, then right again," Mr. Carmichael advised. Zee took a deep breath, looked both ways before walking, looked both ways again, and then followed her family across the street.

They sat for lunch at a local restaurant called Grain and Gather, a farm-to-table-style small eatery with grain bowls and healthy sandwiches served on homemade ceramic plates. The restaurant used organic ingredients and composted their trash. And their fresh juices were ice cold and delicious. "Okay, London's not so bad," Zee said.

As Zee lifted a spoonful of quinoa and tomatoes from her plate to her mouth, her phone buzzed. It was Ally.

Zee stepped away from the table politely before answering. "Ally! *Ohmylanta*, where have you been?!" Zee grilled her.

"Hiii," said Ally in a cautious tone. "So sorry I've been MIA. I've just been a bit preoccupied."

"That's okay! I just got settled here yesterday morning. How are you? How's everything in Paris?"

Zee could hear a loud train sounding through the phone as Ally replied, "It's fine. Can't complain. Liking London?"

Zee's brain was moving a mile a minute. There were so many things she wanted to ask her best friend. *How does she get around all of these crazy, Old World streets? And what's a 'tube'? Do they have tubes in France?*

Zee's questions were met by long silent breaks, as if Ally were doing something else in between sentences. "Oh, yeah, we have a train system here. It's similar..."

"Gosh, I wish we could see each other before I leave for school. What are you up to this week? I have a few days before I have to go to campus."

"What were you thinking?" Ally said.

"I don't know, maybe we could meet somewhere?"

"Oh, I um... I guess I'm free," Ally hesitantly said. "Like maybe Tuesday?"

"Great!" Zee said. "How and where should we meet?"

"Um, well, you can take the train to Paris. It's about two and a half hours from London."

"That's all?!" Zee said excitedly. "Cool! Let me ask my parents and see what day works best."

Zee returned to her family and told her parents about Ally's phone call. "Oh, Paris! I'd love to go to Paris," Mrs. Carmichael said. "But I'll have to go on a solo trip. How am I going to shop and take photos if I have the twins and Zee in tow?"

Zee was growing increasingly annoyed by her mother's new obsession with shopping and documenting herself shopping. "Dad, what's the chance I can go to Paris next week?" she asked.

"By yourself? Slim to none," Mr. Carmichael said. The gray hairs around his temples ("a gift from my precocious children," he often joked) shifted as he clenched and released his jaw. "But because I happen to have a client meeting in Paris this week on Tuesday, I can take you to see Ally. We can make it a day trip and be back home the same night."

Zee threw her arms around her father. "Seriously, Dad? That is beyond cool, thank you!"

"No prob," he said. "Text your pal back and make sure she can meet you at the train station."

Zee fired off a message to her pal and smiled as she continued eating. She looked at her father, nodding her head. "You know, I'm really liking this new job of yours," she said.

3

THE NEW SCHOOL

Zee unpacked half of her bags from California and arranged her things around her room in an orderly manner. She unwrapped a few pictures and awards from Brookdale and hung most of her summer clothes in the closet, leaving a few pairs of shorts and T-shirts toward the front for the last few days of summer. Zee kept the rest of her belongings in the suitcases to take with her to her new school—The Hollows Creative Arts Academy, an arts-focused boarding school located in the Cotswolds.

"As in, I won't be living with you and mom?" Zee had asked a few months ago when her father first told her about The Hollows.

"You can come home on the weekends," said Mr. Carmichael. "Boarding school gives you an amazing education, freedom to be independent and think independently, but also be with other kids your age going through the exact same things. And Jasper will be there too. He went to the Hollows before he came to California."

Zee raised her eyebrows and nodded. *Having Jasper there will be a huge plus*, she thought.

Mr. Carmichael continued, "We thought you would love the creative environment. It's a chance to focus on your music as a critical part of your academics, not just as a side hobby."

Zee had never spent more than a few days away from home at a time and wondered if she'd fit in at her new school. "But I like sleeping at home," Zee said. "Don't you think I'm a bit young to leave home? I can't even drive yet!"

"The best schools in England are often the boarding schools, and they have many more international students than local schools do. We thought you'd meet other kids who might be in your shoes. You know, being an expat."

"An expat," Zee repeated. "That sounds so uncool. Like an old dog that someone left on the side of the road."

"That would be *ex-pet*," said Mr. Carmichael. "Besides, you should be thrilled about your new school. They recycle, ban plastic, and have a Save the Oceans club, just like Brookdale. It'll be just the same but new and exciting, you'll see."

• • •

Realizing she hadn't done much of her own research on the school since they'd arrived in London, Zee popped open her laptop and pulled up the website for The Hollows. A page-wide black-and-white image of several smiling, neatly dressed students gathered on the great lawn was the first impression Zee received. The Hollows looked like a storybook school. The uniforms were perfectly pressed. No one had braces. No one had a hair out of place. *Are these actors?* Zee thought.

The headline at the top of the web page read: *The Hollows: nurturing our children to build a foundation for our future.*

The Hollows was one of the most prestigious boarding schools in the country, particularly known for its environmentally friendly practices and architecture. The campus was LEED certified, and the school claimed that more than eighty percent of the materials used to construct the buildings and structures were eco-friendly. The school was also known for its creative arts programs where students created custom arts concentrations of their own to pursue for their four years. Students were encouraged to be as unique with their concentrations as possible—past studies included classical music for modern times and sustainable culinary arts, or, as one student called it, "Compost Cuisine: Making Five-Star Food from Scraps, Rubbish, and Leftovers."

Zee clicked the menu header that said On Campus, and a page of happy students in uniforms in front of shiny buildings greeted her. *Life at The Hollows—which includes living full time with friends and faculty—is a unique and extraordinary experience*, the introduction read. Photos of smiling upper-level students studying in cozy lounges with foosball tables, wood coffee tables, exposed ductwork, and oversized sofas depicted a happy but academic-focused life at The Hollows.

A section called Arts explained its philosophy on the custom concentrations: *At The Hollows, the creative arts are defined as whatever practice or pursuits allow our students to express their true selves freely and happily.* The campus had more than fifty different arts classes available to them, including dance, music, theater, film photography, creative writing, and culinary arts.

Zee scrolled through photos of their large dance studios, though the students in them looked too pretty and too groomed to be believable. Then Zee's eyes widened when she saw the 8,000-square-meter campus concert hall, which seated 500 people. In addition to the school's annual formals and events, The Hollows often hosted major public concerts by major bands and singers at the hall—both Adele and Ed Sheeran had performed there as rising stars. *I wonder if I will ever play there. Gosh, could I handle that large of a crowd?* Zee wondered.

Zee texted Chloe a link to the school's website with a caption: *My new school looks like a movie set.*

Chloe responded back. *Wow. It's no Brookdale Academy. We're preppy too, but California preppy. Like, chill prep. How many students go there?*

I don't know, but they're all so very adult.

What do the eighth graders look like?

Well, for one, they're not eighth graders. In the U.K., they don't use the same system. Instead of first grade, second grade, etc., they say year one, year two, etc. Eighth grade is called year nine.

Ah, got it, Chloe responded. A minute passed before she texted again. *There's a girl from The Hollows who has a YouTube channel. Izzy Matthews. Her videos look amazing! Perfect hair, perfect teeth, and she has a sick wardrobe. Check out her channel. Maybe this will give you a real sense of the school.*

Zee went to YouTube and typed "Izzy Mathews" into the search bar. Her channel popped up immediately with a playlist of all her recent videos. Blonde-haired, doe-eyed Izzy was originally from the Cotswolds and an incoming year niner at The Hollows. Zee clicked on the latest video, a well-edited ten-minute film of Izzy going from class to the cafeteria to the soccer fields, narrating her moves with fast chatter and hand-drawn captions. Zee watched another video that focused on a creative showcase The Hollows hosted in the fall, and another video of one of Izzy's weekends at home, her English spaniels nipping at her feet while she tossed her hair and giggled. Zee poked around Izzy's YouTube channel for an hour, noting not only how much her friends looked a lot like her, but that she was a pretty good soccer player and had classic novels stacked in her dorm room.

Zee

She's probably the most popular girl at school.

Chloe

Maybe you'll meet her on campus. And maybe you'll get in one of her videos.

Zee

I doubt I'll ever see her!

Chloe

Oh, and maybe you'll become a regular in her videos and you can become YouTube famous too! Don't forget about me once you get "verified."

Zee rolled her eyes and smiled.

> **Chloe, this is me you're talking to. If you want the influencer of the Carmichael family, text my mom.**

Zee looked down at the small numbers on the left side of the screen. Izzy's channel had 50,000 subscribers. *I bet my mom would love her,* Zee thought to herself.

4

FRENCH (DIS)CONNECTION

*T*he chimes of Zee's phone alarm stirred her awake at 6:30 a.m. on Tuesday morning, which would be tough on any day, but the killer jet lag made Zee's head even groggier. She sat up in bed and blinked her eyes open. Then she remembered it was Tuesday. Paris Tuesday.

Zee packed a day bag with an eye mask in case she could catch a nap at some point, her unicorn headphones to listen to music on the train ride, and her journal in which she wrote songs and other deep thoughts. She checked the train schedule once again—her Eurostar train to Paris would leave at 8:15 a.m. Zee showered and put on a pair of slim black capri pants and a striped tee, hoping to look Paris chic for her meetup.

Mr. Carmichael was reading the news on his iPad when Zee came into the kitchen for breakfast. "You excited?" he asked.

"Yeah," she said. "I texted Ally like three times already."

The two had helpings of scrambled eggs, tomatoes, orange juice, and whole-grain bread, finishing up just as Mrs.

Carmichael and the twins joined them around the kitchen table. Then Zee and her father hopped into the Uber waiting for them outside and headed for the train station.

"I'm glad I'm the one who gets to take you to Paris first," said Mr. Carmichael.

"Really?" said Zee.

"Well, with the move and all, I feel like we haven't had that much time together. And I wanted to take you on my first work trip. This is a small work trip, but it's still Paris."

"What *are* you doing in Paris today?" Zee asked.

"Today we're meeting with Aston Martin about becoming their ad agency. We are pitching their marketing team ideas for a new campaign."

"Oh, wow! Yeah, they have been using the same old dude in their ads for, like, ever."

Suddenly, Zee's phone vibrated. A notification from Ally lit up the screen but darkened Zee's mood.

Ally

> Zee, so sorry to do this, but I have to cancel our meetup today. Something came up. So sorry. Call you later.

A lump started to swell in Zee's throat. *Really, Ally? Right when I need you the most?* Zee thought.

"Oh man," Zee said. "Ally bailed on me."

"Really?" Mr. Carmichael said. "Now?"

Zee's face grew sullen. "I can't believe she would just bail with no explanation. What could possibly be that important?"

"Sir, can you pull over for just a sec? We might have a

change in plans," Mr. Carmichael told the Uber driver. Then he looked at the car's dashboard clock. "Well, we have two options. If you still want to see Paris, you could come with me. We're almost at the train station, and I'd love to take you to the Eiffel Tower after my meeting. Or I can take you back home and take a later train, no problem. Up to you."

Zee felt a knot in her chest. She had been relying on her visit with Ally to boost her self-esteem a few days before she was due to leave for boarding school. Now she felt so lost. "Paris can wait for me, Dad. Would you mind taking me home?"

"Sure," he said. "Wanna stop for a scone on the way back?"

"It's okay," Zee said. She felt a pit in her stomach so large, there's no way there'd be room for any food.

• • •

As the Uber with Mr. Carmichael still in the backseat pulled away from the street and back toward the train station, Zee slinked inside her family's new home. She tossed her bag in defeat onto the floor by the door. Her mother, who was upstairs walking from the twins' bedroom down the hall, spotted Zee as she came in through the door. "Honey, what happened?"

"Ally bailed on me," Zee said. "Texted me at the last minute that something came up."

"What?" replied Mrs. Carmichael. "That's a bit worrisome. You didn't want to go to Paris with your father?"

"Nah, I was looking forward to seeing Ally."

Mrs. Carmichael looked beyond Zee. "Well, sorry to hear all this, dear. You have a package in the kitchen."

Zee walked through the kitchen entry and looked on the

counter for those yummy chocolate biscotti her mom snagged from the local market when she did the first grocery haul. Then Zee saw the big package on the kitchen table with a label with her name on it. The return address was from The Hollows.

Zee ripped open the brown paper wrapping and uncovered a black leather clothing box wrapped in red ribbon. Zee cut the ribbon and opened the lid. There was a stack of tightly folded, crisp white button-down shirts and a few wide-pleated navy skirts, plus a gray cardigan and a navy blazer, both with school emblems on the breast pockets.

Uniforms, Zee thought. She never did well with uniforms. Brookdale Academy also required them, but they consisted of a crew neck vest or polo shirt and a navy skirt, giving students plenty of room to wear whatever shirts, jackets, and accessories they wanted to. Given Zee's thick, curly red hair, scattered dark freckles, olive skin, and blue eyes, looking like other people was never going to happen no matter what uniform she wore. Zee opened up the packaging for one white shirt and one skirt. She held the pieces to the window light. *These look... expensive*, she thought.

An envelope addressed to "Mackenzie" fell out from between the folds of the wrapping. The stationery felt just as luxe as the clothes. Zee opened it and found a note from the uniform's designer, Misha Nonoo.

Mackenzie,

    It's an honor to design your uniforms for The Hollows. I hope they help you feel strong, confident, and empowered, no matter what your school days entail. These pieces are designed to be mixed and matched to make twenty stylish looks. All are made with high-quality sustainable fabrics that feel good to wear and will last all four seasons. If you need any assistance with styling or care of the uniforms, please let me know and I'd be happy to help.

Best,

Misha Nonoo

Zee carried the package and the clothes upstairs to her room, where her mother stood with a tape measure and a finger to her chin. "What are you doing?" Zee asked.

"Just taking some measurements," said Mrs. Carmichael. "I think I want to get you some new furniture."

"What's wrong with the stuff I have?" Zee asked. "I love my bed. We sanded down the wood of that frame for two days together."

"Yes, because we got it secondhand at an estate sale in Brentwood, which was great at the time. But now I think I want to give you something a bit more elevated for your new London home."

"The home that I won't even see much of because I'm going to boarding school," Zee said.

"Gone, but not forgotten, darling."

Again with the "darling," Zee thought to herself.

"Are those your uniforms?" Mrs. Carmichael said, dropping the tape measure. "If they don't fit, I'll have to send them back for different sizes. You don't want to look sloppy on your first day of school, do you? Can you put on the blazer?"

Zee reluctantly let her mother put the blazer over her vintage concert tee and her reclaimed Japanese denim jeans. The blazer was comfortable, the sleeves falling to the first knuckle of her thumb. "Oh good, nice and snug in the shoulders," Mrs. Carmichael said, smiling. "How do you feel?"

Zee walked over to the mirror against the far corner wall. She took in her reflection from the top of her curly-haired head to the bottom of the seam of the jacket. Then she reached down and smoothed the jacket. The material, the softest fabric

she'd ever had in a jacket, felt soothing under her fingertips. She felt herself stand up slightly taller, more confident. She smiled. "I feel like I'm going to a board meeting, not school," said Zee. "It's a good thing."

• • •

Ally bailed on me, Zee texted Chloe after dinner with her family. Her father brought croissants and a handful of pastries back from La Patisserie, a famous Parisian baker, for dessert. *How very unlike her.*

That is surprising! Chloe texted back. *What's eating her?*

No idea. She wouldn't say. Only that something came up.

On a day you're planning to travel from London to meet her? Weird, Chloe responded. *How are you otherwise?*

Nervous. I leave for school in two days.

Zee thought back to the first day of school in years past. New pens and pencils. New notebooks that she would adorn with stickers and hand lettering. Crisply ironed clothes and brand-new, sparkling white sneakers. Happy reunions with her friends on campus. Even after a summer-long break, things always felt familiar on the first day of school at Brookdale. Now, the only thing familiar to Zee on the first day of school will be... Jasper.

That's better than nothing, Zee thought.

5

ON CAMPUS

On a clear Monday morning, with birds chirping and a warm breeze in the air, Zee arrived at The Hollows campus with her parents and enough clothes and school supplies for the semester.

The Hollows sat on a hundred acres of groomed countryside in the Cotswolds, the campus an architecturally innovative mix of manicured lawns, lush organic gardens, and impeccable buildings made out of reclaimed wood and recycled steel, a nod to the school's environmentally friendly initiatives. The sports complex housed an Olympic-sized swimming pool to host meets and classes, track and field facilities, and soccer, lacrosse, tennis, and basketball courts. The dorms were divided by age. All students stayed the entire week at the school. Trips home were permitted, but the school believed the campus environment fostered more independence and so limited the number of visits during the first term to just two.

Past the sports complex was one of the larger cafeterias

on campus, and just beyond that was a large greenhouse and gardens, where they grew their own vegetables and fruits for the cafeteria. The Hollows had a culinary arts program to teach students how to grow and cook food. Those who studied culinary arts could apprentice at restaurants nearby, such as Soho Farmhouse's Pen Yen. Last year, the school had arranged a trip to Denmark to observe a weekend at a Michelin-starred restaurant in Copenhagen.

Zee nervously peered out the window as they drove up to the year nine girls' dorm on the north end of campus.

"Oh Zee, look! There's the concert hall," Mrs. Carmichael said, pointing to a concrete and glass structure that looked more like a spaceship than a school theater. Mrs. Carmichael turned her attention back to her phone to type a message to the babysitter they had hired for the day to watch the twins while they took Zee to school.

Zee wiped her damp palms on her denim jumpsuit. She was nervous about leaving her parents, but excited about what she'll find on campus. New people? Good food? Interesting subjects and schoolwork? Who knows? She looked out the car window for students who seemed like they might be just as nervous as she was.

The Uber turned right, veering up toward the dorm, and pulled into a car park. "We're here," said Mr. Carmichael. Zee's stomach flipped and flopped. But she put on a smile and got out of the car.

• • •

After lugging two oversized suitcases up a flight of stairs and through a well-lit hallway, Zee opened the door to her room, her parents right behind her. Inside, a slim, dark-haired girl was standing between two beds. The girl turned her head, her silky hair twirling behind her like a veil, her eyes wide, her mouth pursed together. She looked Zee up and down. Then she turned her body fully toward her roommate. "You must be Mackenzie. Pleasure."

"Oh, call me Zee! All my friends do!"

"Call you... Zed? Like the alphabet letter?"

"Yep! Really, it's cool," Zee said, nervously smiling. Her mind drew a blank as she stood in front of her roommate. "Um... I'm sorry, I don't remember..."

"Jameela," the girl said. "Jameela Chopra. JA-Mee-LA."

"Got it. Thanks," Zee said. She gestured to her parents. "This is my mom and dad."

Jameela politely nodded at them. "Hello, pleasure," she said.

"I tried calling you a few times over the summer, but your line was always busy."

"Oh right, yes, so sorry," said Jameela, fishing through her purse for her cell phone. "We were in the countryside and then in Switzerland to visit family and I had horrible mobile reception. But yes, I know you called. Thanks for trying."

"I thought we'd have a chance to meet each other before we arrived on campus."

"Well, now here we are," Jameela said, sitting on the tidy bed against the far wall. "Oh, I've chosen the bed on the east wall because I meditate in the mornings and need to be facing the sunrise. Hope you don't mind."

"Nope, not at all. I will certainly be sleeping when you're meditating."

"Right," Jameela said, looking at her bed. "You're from California, right? I've visited Los Angeles a few times."

"Yes! Did you like it?"

"I was there for a ballet competition, so I didn't see much of the city. We were there to dance."

Zee looked at Jameela's bed, dressed in a bright white embroidered down comforter and two large down pillows with silk pillowcases. She had already decorated her desk with her laptop, a candle, and a small desk lamp. A pair of pointe shoes hung over her lamp. "Those were my first pair of pointe shoes. I won the Junior Smalls competition with those shoes," Jameela said.

"Wow," Mrs. Carmichael said.

Zee looked out the window in between the two beds and saw the room faced the courtyard. She could see other students hugging and excitedly chatting, catching up like old friends who hadn't seen each other in months. She remembered those types of hugs she had with Ally or Chloe, and longed for them now. Jameela seemed like the type who had not hugged anyone in some time.

Mr. and Mrs. Carmichael wanted Zee to be as independent as possible, so they helped unpack the organizer unit for underneath her bed and hung a few larger framed pictures, and left the rest for Zee to finish and set up her room on her own later. Zee unzipped her suitcase and placed her journal on the bed. She pulled out the navy blazer and the three button-down shirts for her uniform, shaking them out before hanging them in her closet.

"Looks like you're going to need an iron," Jameela said right before she walked out of the room.

Zee nodded. "Yeah, any chance you..." But Jameela was gone.

Zee turned her head back to her clothes. She cast a glance toward Jameela's closet and noticed five perfectly pressed blazers, white button-down shirts, and pleated skirts hanging neatly in her closet. Zee sighed, wondering which would wrinkle first—Jameela's crisp uniform, or her crisp personality.

After an hour of Zee and her parents wandering campus before returning to the dorm, it was finally time for Zee's parents to say goodbye. Zee walked them out to the stairs that led to the exit. The Carmichaels hugged their daughter tightly. Zee fought back tears, sad about her parents leaving her to fend for herself at school, anxious about the unpacking ahead of her. But look at this campus. Look at her roommate, beautiful and posh. *If boarding school created mature students like Jameela, then surely it's not that bad of an institution,* Zee thought. *Right?*

Mrs. Carmichael put her hands on her daughter's nervous face. "We're just a phone call away. Or a text, or a DM. You need anything, we're here."

Mr. Carmichael squeezed Zee's hand. "Call us whenever you need."

Zee nodded, turning her gaze to the floor. Her parents backed away from Zee slowly and headed down the hall, waiting for their daughter to go back inside of her room before Mrs. Carmichael wiped tears away with her scarf.

• • •

The roommates spent the late morning unpacking, organizing, setting up laptops to the campus server, and signing up for the weekly laundry service that picked up their dorm's laundry every Friday morning. Even dirty laundry was washed with eco-friendly methods—the washers all had water sensors that calculated the most efficient amount of water and detergent to use per load.

By the time they finished unpacking, it looked like two completely different people took up the space. Zee's bed was covered by a brand-new textured duvet her mother picked out (though Zee had been fine with the hand-crocheted blanket she had on her bed at home) with several colorful pastel pillows on top. A large map of the world covered the wall above her bed.

Pictures of her friends and family sat in frames stacked on her desk, and she put one photo of her and Ally on her dresser, next to her collection of journals. She stuffed her clothes into the five dresser drawers the school provided. Her hair products took up most of the top of her dresser, and several pairs of eyeglasses laid beside them.

Jameela's side of the room was sparse. No photos of friends from home. None even of her parents. There were very few books on her shelves aside from her textbooks for school and a few ballet schedules. Her headphones, computer, and two Smythson notebooks were neatly arranged on the desk, along with a small makeup bag and a few Grayson pens. Her dresser had a hairbrush, a compact, a few lipsticks, and an expensive-looking tube of mascara. Her shower caddy leaned next to the dresser.

Each dorm had its own cafeteria, but for lunch and dinner, most students gathered in the larger dining halls so they could hang out with friends of the opposite sex and older students who lived in other dorms. Zee's stomach growled. She had already eaten all of the yummy snacks Chloe had given her from their last sleepover.

Jameela disappeared for a few minutes before returning to their room, her hair freshly brushed through and even glossier in the midday light. She was wearing her uniform jacket, a perfectly fitted white boyfriend button-down, and Alexander McQueen sneakers, though classes didn't begin for another few days.

"Do I need to wear my uniform, even if there are no classes?" asked Zee.

"The usual rule is uniforms are worn Monday through

Friday, but on the weekends we can go casual. I believe because there are no classes today they're not required, just encouraged," Jameela said. "Shall we have some lunch? I'm peckish."

Zee reached for her school blazer hanging in her closet and smoothed it over with her hand before putting it on, and they headed out.

· · ·

Jameela and Zee walked side by side across campus under the warm August sun. The ballerina's long legs strode effortlessly through the wide greenspace between buildings, and it seemed she walked on her toes even outside of a dance studio. Jameela looked straight ahead as Zee, taking two steps for each of her roommate's steps, gushed about her excitement for her classes.

On the way to the dining hall, upper-level students rode by on bicycles and yelled greetings to each other. Zee looked up at the modern design on the buildings. Although they all were made of concrete and steel and glass, it seemed as if the buildings disappeared into the natural surroundings, mirroring the sky, the trees, and the birds singing...

Wham!

"Ugh!" Zee said as she slammed face first into a taller, slim, sharply dressed boy.

"Oy! Watch yourself there," he said, slightly annoyed.

They locked eyes, and his face softened. Zee was stunned by the sheer beauty of the boy's green eyes, square jaw, and sun-kissed cheeks.

"I'm sorry, I didn't see you... I mean, obviously. I'm sorry."

The boy smirked and looked at Zee, from her full, curly red hair to her blue eyes behind wire-framed glasses, to her now rumpled blazer, to her white sneakers she customized with rhinestones around the rubber trim and the V logo on the side.

"Nice trainers," he said, and winked as he walked off.

Jameela peered at her with a judgmental squint of the eye. "Do you know who that was?" she hissed.

"Someone who I almost gave a black eye to?" Zee said.

"That, my dear, was Archie Saint John. Spoiled rich kid, descended from aristocracy, private-plane-flying, genetically blessed Archie Saint John. He is the hottest guy on campus."

"The entire campus?"

"Well, definitely within year nine. But I challenge anyone to dispute me."

"Are you two friends?"

"Not necessarily. Archie doesn't have friends. He has acquaintances. Says friends are too much work. Or at least that's his excuse. Keeps people at arm's length. He's also into music. Writes songs, plays guitar. Oh, he's also very stylish. Like more than most guys. And"—she looked at Zee's sneakers—"some girls."

"Huh," Zee said, processing the information. "Well, at least he didn't embarrass me after I embarrassed him."

"Indeed," Jameela said. The two arrived at the dining hall and walked inside.

6

BREAKING BREAD

*T*he spacious, sunlight-drenched dining hall ran on solar power and sourced all of its food from the large organic garden on campus, run in part by students and the school's horticulture team. The school was proud to accommodate all types of dietary preferences—gluten-free, dairy-free, vegetarian, vegan, organic, non-GMO, and paleo. Thankfully, students could still source peanut butter if they went to a special kiosk at the back of the hall.

The savory smell of garlic and butter permeated the large room as Zee walked by the large menu board at the front of the entrance to the food stations. She read aloud the neatly written text. "Todays specials: roasted root vegetable shepherd's pie, bangers and mash... what's a banger?"

"Like sausage," Jameela said. "Mash is mashed potatoes."

"Ooh, vegan chili!" Zee lit up. "That sounds yummy!"

"It's so warm out and you're going to eat chili?" Jameela said. "I want a salad."

Jameela walked away, leaving Zee in front of three

steaming pots of meaty-ish chilis. She weighed her options—a mushrooms and zucchini version, another with spicy red pepper and Chipotle and cotija cheese, and a traditional option—and put a finger to her mouth.

A voice piped up from behind her. "I'm going for the red pepper one. I like spice."

Zee turned to see a boy with mala beads hanging from his neck, arm stacked with leather and beaded bracelets, and a jacket worn inside out and covered with patches that looked like passport stamps. He placed his hand on his chest and introduced himself formally. "Tom Anand. Are you new here? I don't think I saw you last year."

"Zee," she replied, smiling. "Yes, I just got here this morning."

"Then you must be starving," Tom said. "Get a large bowl. And don't forget the roll. You like spicy food too?"

"Um, no. I think I'll go with the standard vegan option."

"Yes! Save the cows," Tom said. "Moooo!"

Zee giggled. "Are you in..."

"Year nine."

"Oh! Just like me."

"Yeah? Well, welcome."

"Thanks. I transferred here this year from California," Zee said. "My dad got a new job."

"Ah cool. I'm used to that," Tom said, grabbing a bowl of Mexican vegan chili. "My parents write books, so we're always moving around for their projects. I actually missed the last part of the school year because we moved to Dubai for my mom's latest book she was researching. We just got back two nights ago."

"Whoa!" Zee said. "Aren't you, like, tired?"

"Nah. I slept well the last two days, and I don't get jet lag. I follow a clean diet. Keeps my body cycle running smoothly."

"And you know this at thirteen?"

"Yes! Well, efficiently for now, I guess. I tweak it depending on what I'm doing. Like if I'm traveling, you know."

"Right." Zee spooned her chili into a large bowl and pushed the tray down the counter toward the vegetables. "Oh, almost forgot my roll," she said.

"Right," Tom replied, smiling. "Oh, and pass on the peas. Always pass on the peas. But they do all right with the asparagus. I'm grabbing a few spears."

The two walked toward the cashier and scanned their ID cards, their main form of payment on campus. Zee spotted Jameela just past the register at the condiment station, drizzling a light dressing on what looked like a trough of greens. Tom followed Zee out, not heading anywhere, but not walking away.

"Jameela! Are you coming to sit?" Zee asked as she walked over.

Jameela looked at Tom, puzzled. "So you're back."

Tom looked at Jameela, annoyed. "Yup. As are you."

Zee looked at them both, confused. She was hungry, both for lunch and to know why these two had this awkward rapport between them. It was like they'd kissed during a game of Truth or Dare and secretly liked it and tried it again in a dark closet somewhere but didn't want anyone to know.

Zee finally broke the silence between them. "Shall we sit for lunch somewhere?"

The three found a table near the large stained-glass window overlooking the garden. Tom and Jameela sat across from one another. Jameela eagerly dived into her mountain of greens with slices of organic chicken, mandarin oranges, and halved almonds. Tom shoveled a spoonful of chili into his mouth and seemingly swallowed each bite, not bothering to chew.

"I take it you guys know each other from last year?" Zee asked, eyeing them both.

"Yes," Jameela said.

"'Know' is a relative term. If you mean to have assumptions about who we are and what we like, then yes. If you mean to have forged a close, respectful relationship with mutual adoration, then nope, never heard of her."

"Your second definition would imply that the subject of said adoration would in fact be worthy of said adoration," Jameela shot back.

Tom looked up from his chili. "May all beings be filled with loving kindness," he said, beginning what sounded like a mantra to show forgiveness toward people who have been unkind.

The chilliness between the two cast a shadow on the lunch table, and just when Zee was about to interrupt this cutting banter, she was distracted by an unmistakable swagger down the aisle. It was the same dark-haired, gorgeous boy Zee had run into, now with a group of boys as they laughed and pointed fingers. They had warm sandwiches in their hands and two of the guys carried trays. Archie paused and looked around for a spot, and the boys made their way to the open table across from Zee, Jameela, and Tom. The table had room for four there, but they were five people, and there was an open spot right next to Tom, across from Zee, with just enough room for Archie to sit.

"Well, well, just my luck, eh?" Archie said as he looked at Zee. "Is this spot taken?"

"No. Please," she said, motioning her hand to the seat. "I'll try not to tackle you this time."

Archie, amused, smiled at her. He nodded to Jameela and Tom. "Welcome back, everyone."

"Archie," Tom greeted.

"Hello, Archie," Jameela said, her voice dropping in pitch. She shook her head to give just enough movement to her lush black locks to create a frame around her thin, heart-shaped face.

Archie unwrapped his sandwich and turned his attention to the boys at the next table. One by one, they dove into their lunches, a quiet hush falling over the group as they ate. Archie looked back to his lunch, and then at the glittery objects below the table.

"Those trainers," he said. "Are those custom?"

"Yes," Zee said. "I made them myself."

"I see," Archie said. He was wearing bright white leather sneakers that looked more appropriate for a business meeting than a basketball court. "I do like someone who flies in the face of convention."

Zee half-smiled, crossing one foot over the other.

"I don't think we formally met the last time we spoke. I'm Archie. Archie Saint John."

Archie held out his hand, waiting for Zee to return the gesture.

"Zee."

"Zee? Is that short for something?"

"Yes, Mackenzie."

"Mmm, Mackenzie. Lovely. I like Mackenzie. The more syllables in your name, the more intrigue there is in the person. Right, Jameela?"

Jameela blushed, sopping up Archie's compliments like a pancake on syrup. "Absolutely."

"What kind of nonsense theory is that?" Tom retorted.

Archie smiled and took a sip of his ice water. "Archie's law."

"Is Archie your full name?" Zee asked.

"I am Archibald Saint John the Fourth, but really that's a mouthful to write on my forthcoming album covers, so I go by Archie. Better stage name anyway."

"Ah, do you play in a band or something?"

"I am a singer, songwriter, one-man band."

Zee felt like she found a kindred spirit. "Me too!" she blurted. "I'm Mackenzie Blue Carmichael."

"Blue?" Archie says. "Your middle name is really Blue?"

"I'm from California," Zee says. "Cool names come with the territory."

Jameela rolled her eyes. "Zee just transferred here. This is her first year at The Hollows. And at boarding school in general."

Archie perked up. "Cali, eh? Ah, that's wicked! A lot of my inspiration comes from West Coast artists."

"Right," Zee said. "You do have a few great bands here too, like the Rolling Stones and the Beatles."

"Yeah, but they're a bit older, ya know? Not my groove."

Archie turned toward the boys. Jameela gave Zee a glance and carefully dabbed at the corners of her mouth with her napkin. Then she sat up taller, staring directly at Archie's mouth while he bantered with his friends at the next table. Meanwhile, Tom took out a book on chakra healing, which was dog-eared and highlighted already. He hummed something to himself as he read.

"Is that for a class?" Zee asked him.

"Nope. It's for my meditation practice. I write my own. I studied with Deepak Chopra when I was eleven," Tom said. "I'm not just on YouTube following whoever some girl on Instagram said was cool." He looked at Jameela with a steely gaze.

Jameela stood up. "Namaste, Tom. I'm off to the stationers. I need a few folders for class. Zee, I'll see you back at the dorms later. Good luck."

Zee gave her a half-smile as Jameela left before turning back to Tom. "What's with you two?"

Tom shrugged his shoulders. "I've known her since we were four. We went to the same Montessori school in Cambridge, then my parents moved around for work and I've been back and forth ever since. Jameela's been here in the U.K., in Cambridge for a bit, and now at The Hollows, and her view on the world is quite singular. Ya know?"

"No, I don't know," Zee said. "I've only known her for half a day."

Zee looked down at her chili, growing more worried about the thought of spending an entire school year with Jameela. *She's tense, she doesn't eat much, she's very serious about ballet,* Zee thought. *What if I want to stay up late writing songs or have video chats with my friends—is she going to freak out about that?*

"Well, she can be quite judgmental, but don't let that bother you. She only knows what she knows, and in the grand scheme of this wide world of ours, that's not much," Tom said.

Zee laughed. "Well, I can't say I know that much more," she said. "This is my first year at boarding school."

Archie, who had already finished his sandwich, whipped his head back toward Zee. Zee quickly looked away, slightly embarrassed that she spoke loud enough for him to hear her. He looked at her wide eyes, then looked at her red hair, her freckles scattered across her face, and the way she twisted her lip, like she was trying to hold in some other revealing facts about herself. He smiled, gathered his belongings and used plates from lunch, and rose from the table.

He leaned over toward Zee. "Your first year is your best

year, mate," he said. "Just you wait."

Archie's friends also rose from their seats and followed him as he walked toward the exit. Halfway down the aisle, the singing and songwriting, well-dressed Archibald Saint John the Fourth turned back to Zee and gave her a wink.

7

SCHOOL DAZE

*T*he first day of school began at 7 a.m. for Zee, but for Jameela it started much earlier. Zee woke up to see her roommate already gone. With one eye open, Zee looked out the window and saw a beautiful well-kept lawn and teachers starting to make their way to their classes.

Jameela returned dressed in a beautiful set of cotton Desmond & Dempsey pajamas, her long, silky hair tied up in a loose bun. "Morning," she said politely, nothing more.

"Good morning!" Zee said. "How long have you been up?"

"Since 5:30 a.m. I like to meditate and read before I get out of bed. It helps me start my day more focused."

"Wow," Zee said. "Do you get your mediations from Tom? And I didn't hear a thing."

"No, and of course not. Who could hear anything over your snoring?"

"I don't snore," Zee said.

"Oh? Maybe that's just a sinus problem?"

Zee flushed, her cheeks hot. She sleepily rose out of bed and reached for her toiletry basket, did a quick check in the mirror, and slipped her feet into her fluffy slippers before opening the door and heading to the bathroom. Another student was coming out of the bathroom just as Zee approached.

"Oh sorry!" the girl said, looking down as she sidestepped around Zee. "Ooh, I use that body wash, it's great! From the States, yes?"

"Um, yes, it's from my favorite shop back at home," Zee said. The blonde girl looked familiar. And sounded familiar. Where had Zee seen her before? Zee locked eyes with her and saw the largest blue eyes she'd ever seen. It was Izzy Matthews. YouTube star. Boarding school student. And now, apparently, Zee's floormate.

"Oh! You're from the States? Whereabouts?" Izzy perked up.

"California," Zee replied.

"Oh, that's my favorite! Are you from L.A.? I spent some time there over the summer. I love The Grove. All those stores and that ice cream shop is to die for."

"Yes. It's the best. Their chocolate butterscotch is my favorite flavor!"

"Right! Where's your room?"

"Down there, second on the right."

"Awesome, great to run into you. I'm Izzy, by the way."

"Zee," Zee replied. "Short for Mackenzie."

"Right! Ha, we're practically related. See you around!"

Zee was gobsmacked. The most popular YouTube boarding school vlogger called her a sister. And she loved California! And she smelled like strawberries, and that was before the shower! *Maybe I will get to be in one of her videos,* Zee thought to herself.

Zee took a quick shower with the recycled rainwater that the school collected, filtered, and ran throughout campus. She quickly brushed her teeth and washed and moisturized her face with her favorite Florence by Mills products, then returned to her room to get dressed. Jameela was perched over her laptop, reading e-mails and scribbling into her notebook.

"I met Izzy Matthews in the shower," Zee blurted.

"Really," Jameela sniffed. "You couldn't give the poor girl some privacy?"

"No, geez," Zee scoffed. "I mean I met her on the way to the bathroom, in the hallway."

"Right," said Jameela. "Miss Izzy. She is a boarding-school lifer."

"Yes, I gathered from her YouTube channel."

"She tried to get me on that thing and now I have to run for cover every time. She brings her camera everywhere and I'm always telling her, 'Darling, can we please just have some breakfast without an iPhone in my oatmeal?'"

It was the funniest thing Jameela had said since Zee arrived. Cracking a giggle, Zee slipped on a white shirt and a pleated navy skirt around her hips, tucking the long ends of the shirttail inside. To add some much-needed flair to the look, she put on mismatched striped socks with her sneakers. "Do we need our blazer for breakfast? It's a bit warm outside."

"Yes. We have assembly and a meeting right after. You need your blazer on at all times. It's part of the full uniform look."

Zee begrudgingly slid her arms into the armholes of her navy jacket, grabbed her bag, and followed Jameela out the door.

• • •

After grabbing breakfast in the dorms, a barrage of navy-jacketed students swarmed the great hall and scattered for seats for the school's first assembly of the term. Jameela and Zee found an area designated for year nine students and slid in a few rows in front of Archie and his crew. Zee gave him a nod as she took her seat. He looked her way and smirked. Jameela mistakenly took his gaze for her, and she smiled broadly.

Just as they settled in, Zee's phone buzzed. She had two text messages, one of which was from her parents wishing her a fantastic first day of school. The other was from Chloe.

Chloe

Hey girl. Show those London boarders the beauty of California. You're going to kill it at school today. Text me later and tell me everything. XOXO.

"You should shut that off before assembly starts. You're not allowed to have your phone on in class," Jameela warned.

"Right," Zee responded. She typed fast into the keyboard, sending caramel-skinned fist bump emojis to the both of them, and turned the phone off.

Headmaster Shane Smythe, a tall man with a bald head and glasses, took the stage and gave a bellowing welcome speech to the entire student body. He welcomed new students arriving to The Hollows for the first time this year, and then ran through important dates for the term period, including the most competitive all-campus event of the year, the Creative Arts Festival. "This year's festival will be held in November," he announced.

"Oh yes!" Zee whispered. "I'm so in. I always participated in my old school's talent festival."

Jameela leaned toward her. "This festival isn't just your run-of-the-mill talent fest. It's a grand showcase, an audition in front of real agents and scouts from the U.K.'s biggest television networks, film studios, and dance academies."

"Really?"

"Yeah. Some students have landed on television shows and in movies simply from their performances at the Fest."

"Well, I ended up on a TV show after performing at my old

school's talent show," Zee said.

Jameela's eyes jumped in surprise. "Well, then you'll be ready for this level of competition."

Suddenly Zee felt a pang of anxiety. Sure, her writing and songs were great, and she even landed a Hollywood agent for her talent. But what if the Brits don't get it? What if they don't get *her*?

Zee looked across the crowd. She hadn't yet seen her buddy Jasper, who she thought she would have heard from by now, the first day of school. Maybe she'd see him when classes start? Izzy sat a few rows in front of her with her girlfriends, the crew excitedly shaking their heads as if they already knew what they'd do for their Festival performances. Izzy leaned against two of her friends and threw a peace sign while another friend took a selfie, moving quickly so that they wouldn't get caught by the headmaster and have their phones taken away from them.

Tom sat behind them, looking bemused. He'd probably write some poetry for the Festival. Maybe perform a healing sound bath? Jameela would likely perform a classical ballet piece that would undoubtedly be sharp and technical. She'd have it no other way.

Then there was Archie. She turned back to look his way, and saw he was already looking at her. His eyes pierced hers, and she wondered how long he'd been staring at her. She also wondered if that stare meant he already planned his Festival performance—and if it might possibly involve her.

• • •

The rest of the day moved in a blur. From lengthy introductions to new teachers, to a snowstorm of handouts and schedules and term sheets and materials for each class, the school day was packed with activity. *I might need Tom to give me a meditation for peace, kindness, and some passing grades,* Zee thought.

Zee's algebra class was right after assembly, and her teacher there, Mr. Stevens, warned the class there would be pop quizzes every week, unannounced, on a whim. "Spontaneity is the spice of life," Mr. Stevens quipped.

Sciences came after math (or "maths," as noted in Zee's school materials). Science was one of Zee's top subjects at Brookdale as it focused on the environment and geography, which she was very interested in. But this term's first subject in science focused on circuitry—the connectivity of electricity, currents, magnetic waves, or basically how things worked. Goodness, her old pal Jasper would love this.

After a quick morning break, Zee went to English comprehension and literature, where students would learn about the great British authors and critique different types of writing, from speeches to technical writing. Zee was stoked for this one. She loved reading and had always done well in English literature given her creative background.

After English she had a "Skills for Life" class, which centered around home economics–type classes that rotated every term. Students studied a mix of culinary arts, sewing, automotive, and computers. Culinary arts was up first for Zee, and she was excited about cooking. Zee and her mother used to cook together in L.A. usually for Sunday brunch, with Zee helping her with pancakes or scrambled eggs while Mrs. Carmichael made the coffee and more complicated dishes. Since the move to London though, they barely had time to sit for a meal together, much less cook one together. In fact, Zee wasn't sure if her mom even had a chance to unpack all of the pots and pans in the kitchen before Zee had left for boarding school.

The afternoon schedule was much better—Zee's arts classes were after lunch. The Hollows required all students starting from year nine to declare their artistic concentration for the year by the end of the second week of school. The artistic concentration was centered around each student's creative talent or interest and each student would then follow a track of study within that concentration. Zee decided to study music with a concentration in songwriting. She was the lead singer of her old band The Beans at Brookdale, and though Zee could play a few notes on a piano, she loved songwriting, enhanced by a vivid imagination and the ability to drift into a dreamlike state anywhere—including her music theory classroom.

Zee's afternoon schedule included an intro to art history class, followed by her music theory class which focused on jazz of the twentieth century during the first term. She was stoked for the class because her father loved jazz and had first introduced Zee to his favorites during long car rides together in California. She smiled as she thought about one of their trips to Malibu, when her dad played jazz the entire way while Zee and her older brother, Adam, made up their own silly lyrics to the mellow instrumentals.

Three minutes into the lecture on jazz, in the middle of the sweet family memory, someone entered the class and briefly blocked her view of the teacher and the lecture board on the stage. She recognized that thick black hair and sleek black leather jacket from this morning as Archie walked to take a seat behind her. Zee held her breath. *Did he see I was sitting here?* she wondered. She closed her eyes and smiled for a few seconds, then quickly looked around to see if anyone saw her.

Zee's eyes dropped down to her notebook. Her palms were sweaty, she was smiling for no reason, and from the minute that Archie sat down behind her it was suddenly quite challenging to concentrate on her studies.

• • •

After a full day of classes, Jameela went to ballet practice for the rest of the afternoon until dinnertime. The rest of the students went to either sport, "prep"—which was like an organized study hall with teachers present to observe and answer questions—or back to the dorms. Zee came back to her room and popped open her laptop. She had an e-mail from Ally. "Finally," she said aloud. She clicked it open.

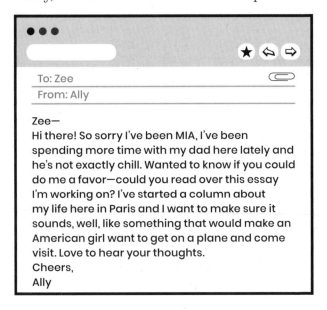

To: Zee
From: Ally

Zee—
Hi there! So sorry I've been MIA, I've been spending more time with my dad here lately and he's not exactly chill. Wanted to know if you could do me a favor—could you read over this essay I'm working on? I've started a column about my life here in Paris and I want to make sure it sounds, well, like something that would make an American girl want to get on a plane and come visit. Love to hear your thoughts.
Cheers,
Ally

Zee stared at the e-mail, searching for any sign of concern or curiosity for Zee's life or her first day at school. *After not speaking to her for a week, after blowing me off for our reunion in Paris, she writes me not to say I'm sorry or to explain herself, but to ask me to read her essay? I mean, she hasn't even texted me!*

Zee looked at her watch—3:15 p.m. She had ten minutes before she had to report to prep, so she quickly opened the attachment to Ally's e-mail and read the essay. The topic: a California girl's first experiences in Paris.

Zee read the first few paragraphs and felt her eyes start to droop from boredom. Or annoyance, she couldn't decide which. As Zee started to make notes, a fire started to burn in her chest. *How is it that my best friend, who was only two hours away, only cared to talk to me about editing her schoolwork?*

8

PILLOW TALK

Though she only had a few minutes before prep, Zee quickly responded to Ally's request. Zee gave her a few edits on her essay, mostly about some punctuation issues, a misspelled word in the third paragraph, and a question about the escargot reference in the last paragraph (specifically, "what is escargot?"). *Hope this helps,* Zee wrote. *And what's going on with your dad?*

A few minutes later Ally wrote back. *Thanks so much! Oh, nothing, we're good. Just spending lots of time together.*

Ah, okay. Where is your mom? Zee asked.

Ally didn't respond immediately. Zee was already running late, so she shut off the phone and headed to prep. A few minutes turned into a few hours, but between studying, dinner with Tom and Jameela, and an impromptu floor hang with her dormmates, Zee expected to hear back from Ally before she went to sleep. But lights out came and went. A reply from Ally never arrived.

• • •

Between algebra and circuitry, Zee's mornings were grueling. Math had never been her strongest subject, but with lots of studying and extra credit, Zee always made above-average marks. She was worried she was never going to understand circuitry, and if she couldn't understand circuitry, she wasn't going to pass her first term of boarding school. She wished her pal Jasper were here. She still hadn't seen him during the first few days. He was a genius with anything involving computers, let alone music. And she liked hanging out with him. She liked how his thick, blonde hair always fell in front of his left eye when he laughed. She... would like to know where the *mylanta* he is!

"Zee!" A perky voice called behind her as Zee was walking to her dorm for a small morning break. Izzy appeared and matched pace with Zee. "Hey! How's your first week? I noticed you weren't feeling our algebra class."

"Why do you say that?" Zee said.

"You spent more time staring out the window than you did at your notes."

"Oh," said Zee, embarrassed. She came up with a quick lie. "I was thinking about a possible song I was going to work on for the Creative Arts Festival."

"Ah, right," said Izzy, waving a hand. "Well, we have some time before Festival. In the meantime, I thought you'd might like to join our study group. My girls and I get together after class every day."

"Really? So you don't play sports after school?"

"No, I still do soccer after class," Izzy said. "We gather

during prep, but we sort of carve out a separate section for ourselves so we're not distracted by others. And we can set up multiple cameras of ourselves studying without bothering anyone else so I can film for my vlog. Wanna come?"

Zee couldn't believe that her study session would be a part of one of YouTube's most popular teen channels. Algebra seemed to be one of Izzy's stronger subjects—her hand shot up to answer all of the questions in class, and she hardly flinched when the professor assigned a pop quiz yesterday. Since writing wasn't one of Izzy's better skills, Zee thought she could help the group by sharing her notes for English lit. Zee wondered if she would be on camera. Should she wear more makeup besides her lip gloss? Do something special with her hair?

"Sure, I'd love to," Zee replied. "But, um, do I have to be on..."

"Great, we'll see you tomorrow!"

Izzy waved as she walked away, her blonde hair whipping around her back as she turned. Zee smiled, happy to have another friend at her new school, especially one who has more than 50,000 friends on the Internet.

• • •

Zee

> Chlo! OMG. So much to tell you! I'm dormmates with that Izzy Matthews girl you put me on to!

Zee texted Chloe back at her dorm room. She had lots to catch her up on: the first day of school, Archie, classes, Izzy.

Zee held her phone in her hand, awaiting a response from her friend. Usually, Chloe responded in seconds, no matter what platform she was on. Nothing.

Zee closed the text app and opened Instagram. She looked at Chloe's feed to see when the last time she posted was. Yesterday afternoon. "Okaaay," Zee said, closing Instagram and opening WhatsApp. It said she was last seen on the app today at 2:30 a.m.

"Two thirty!" Zee said. "Does she sleep?"

And then it hit her—right now, Chloe was asleep. It was 10:10 a.m. in London but eight hours earlier in California. Zee's best friend was in bed, her phone on silent mode for the only time of the day it didn't sing with notifications from her many messages.

"Aw man," Zee said as she put her phone back to silent mode. She grabbed her book for her afternoon classes and headed out.

• • •

Music theory class was definitely Zee's favorite of the term so far. The class curriculum started with the history of jazz. Studying jazz greats was more interesting than she expected, in part because of the extraordinary personal struggles behind singers like Ella Fitzgerald and Louis Armstrong. *Ella worked for the mafia?* Zee wrote in her notes. *MIND. BLOWN.*

Every day, Archie made it to class right as the teacher, Mr. Hysworth, took to the chalkboard, and left right as the clock struck 2:45 p.m., barely giving Mr. Hysworth enough time to finish explaining the homework. It was unclear where exactly

Archie went afterward, but it wasn't to study—Zee had not once seen him in prep, though it was required, nor had she seen him in sport. She wasn't even sure where he lived on campus.

Toward the end of the first week of music theory, Zee was attentively taking notes on the professor's lecture about jazz's African roots. Suddenly, Archie leaned toward her.

"Hey," he whispered. "Are you into this stuff?"

"Yeah, it's fascinating," she replied, nodding. "I think I might work on a jazz song myself. Or"—she suddenly felt inspiration from her own name—"an album: *Mackenzie Sings the Blues*."

Archie smiled, then looked at her notes. "You take a lot of notes. You know what the best way to learn about jazz is? To listen to jazz live."

"Yeah?" Zee said, laughing nervously.

"I know there's a showcase happening at the coffee shop in town by this cool underground bands. Some of them used to go to The Hollows, I reckon. Thinking of going. Wanna come with?"

"What time will it be? It sounds like a late-night thing."

"It's at 9:30 p.m."

"That's past curfew, Archie."

"Not if you're going to do some late-night research in the field, it isn't."

Zee's mouth dropped. "There's no way the headmaster will allow us to leave past curfew."

Archie shrugged his shoulders. "Let's just say I know how to get around here without attracting attention. And you could always lie and say you're ill and have to go to the chemist," Archie said.

Zee looked puzzled. *Chemist?* But then she remembered that was how the British referred to their pharmacies here. "The headmaster literally hands you off to your parents, guardians, or the cops to let you off the campus. If I don't have that, I can't leave school."

"Just tell the headmaster you're with me," Archie replied, his mouth folding into a Cheshire cat grin.

The idea of watching some cool British band with the hottest kid in school sounded like an amazing way to spend a school night. But it also sounded like a heap of trouble, trouble she didn't have the bandwidth for right now.

"Um, I really appreciate the invitation," Zee replied. "But I'm going to pass. Do you know if there are any daytime showcases by this awesome band?"

Archie sniffed. "Pretty sure this is a onetime gig."

The school bell rung, signaling the end of the day. Archie grabbed his notebook and stood up, not bothering to tuck the chair in under the desk. "Maybe next time, Cali. I'll send you a photo from tonight."

• • •

A good night's sleep was on Zee's to-do list for the evening. Her flannel PJs swam around her slim legs and torso. She tucked her long red hair into a loose topknot on top of her head, then wrapped it up in a beautiful silk scarf her mom found in a vintage shop in L.A. a few years ago. Zee brushed her teeth next to Izzy, who was surrounded by two friends, one holding the camera, the other carrying the O ring light to brighten up the bathroom as she filmed a nightly routine video. When Zee returned to her room, Jameela was already passed out in her bed, the covers pulled up tight under her chin, a small noise machine running by her head.

Zee heard a faint buzzing from her dresser. Her phone flashed as photos landed in her inbox. They were from Archie.

The first one was a blurry image of a band on stage at the coffee shop. The caption: *Wish you were here.*

The second message was a short video clip of the band playing jazz music. Zee reached for her headphones and popped them into her ears before she hit play, and heard a bass guitar going *ba dump bum bump* behind a middle-pitched saxophone. Zee bobbed her head to the beat and responded. *Wow, they're great!*

The third message came quickly after: *They're called The Scene. You still have time to meet me here.*

Zee replied: *Dorm advisor just called lights out. I'm in bed.*

Aww, bummer. Would you like a jazzy lullaby to put you to sleep?

It's better than my circuitry homework. Here's my cell number so we can text back and forth. Faster than e-mailing.

Archie set up his phone to record the band's performance live and texted the video clips to Zee so Zee could watch along with him as close to live as possible. The two sent messages back and forth, critiquing the band members and composition of each song. *The drummer is wicked*, Archie wrote. *You should see him. Looks like he's been smoking since birth.*

I like that last track they did. The flute made it so dreamy.

Her fingers are flying across that flute right now, Archie responded.

How did you hear about them? Zee asked.

Friend of a friend, Archie texted. Then he sent a picture of one of the guitar players, a burly, thick-bearded man who looked to be in his mid-thirties. *That's my friend. He's played with major bands on tours for decades.*

How do you know each other?

Instagram. He posts about vintage guitars. Cool dude.

Zee hadn't had such a detailed discussion about music with someone since she landed at The Hollows and she was excited to find someone as nerdy about the subject as she was. She didn't think in a million years that Archie Saint John would be that someone.

But tonight, after an hour's worth of messages, music had sparked a friendship between two kids from opposite ends of the world. Zee downloaded the band's album to her phone and continued texting Archie until her eyelids grew heavy, a smile sliding across her face as she fell asleep.

9

SLEEPY ZEE

Zee turned over in bed, groggy from a lack of sleep. Her phone lay next to her head, nearly out of battery, but with several notifications for a few missed texts from Archie wishing her a good night. Zee rubbed her eyes into focus, and once they did, she saw a cross-legged Jameela sitting on her bed, already reading through her notes for her first class.

"Morning, sleepyhead," Jameela said. "I see you had a late night yesterday."

Zee propped herself up and out of bed. "I was up talking to Archie all night."

"Archie?" Jameela questioned. "What on earth were you two talking about?"

"He snuck off campus to see a band at the coffee shop, and then texted me during the entire performance to share it with me."

"You texted all night with Archie?" Jameela asked.

Zee grabbed her phone and scrolled through her text messages. She looked at the timestamps of Archie's messages.

"Yes, until 11:37 p.m. apparently, when I must have fallen asleep because I texted 'Gofd nitttt, jazzy..aifoajor.' My face must have fallen flat on the keypad."

Jameela looked at Zee as if she didn't believe her. "He had your number?"

"He e-mailed me at first, since all of our e-mails are in the school directory online. Then I gave him my cell phone number so we could text. The messages could come through faster that way."

Jameela's surprised expression became a smile, spreading across her face as if she'd just eaten the most delicious dessert. "You two basically had a virtual date," said Jameela. "Unbelievable."

"It wasn't a date," Zee said, blushing. "I actually turned him down when he asked me to go with him!"

"But then you watched the band together anyway."

"He watched. I listened via Whatsapp."

"Close enough," Jameela smirked. "You went on a date with Archie Saint John."

Zee rolled her eyes. "I don't think he'd agree." She didn't know what Archie would call what they did last night, and she really didn't know how to summarize it either. But she knew one thing—she'd really like to do it again.

Zee went to the bathroom and cleaned herself up. She brushed her teeth, her toothpaste drooling out of one side of her mouth as she thought about her text message date with Archie. She wondered what they would say to one another when they saw each other again. Should she play it cool? Should she suggest some bands she liked? What if he didn't like her taste? What if he forgot about their exchange already? What should she do? *I know,* Zee thought, *I'll text Ally and Chloe.*

Zee returned to her room and grabbed her phone from her desk. She opened Whatsapp and texted Chloe: *Chlo, OMG last night was...*

Then she looked at the time. She counted backward until she had eight fingers on her hand. "Ugh, this time difference is killing me!" said Zee.

So Zee reached out to Ally, who was in the same time zone and would at least be awake. Ally hadn't responded to her yet after the critique of her personal essay for that literary journal.

Zee

Hey, you around? Much to discuss!

Zee placed the phone on the dresser and continued getting dressed. A flutter grew in her stomach, which could have been a craving for pancakes, or could have been a nervousness for how the day would unfold today. *What if I see Archie this morning?* she thought.

"You ready for breakfast?" Jameela asked.

Zee and Jameela shuffled to the cafeteria. Both grabbed an apple and Zee made herself a bowl of oatmeal and topped it off with crushed pecans and coconut. She sipped on Earl Grey tea, hoping the caffeine would help her shake the groggies. Jameela ate only the apple and washed it down with a warm cup of tea. "Maybe you can catch a nap during morning break," Jameela said, before walking off toward the quad ahead of Zee.

• • •

Classic literature. Sure, it was popular in the olden days, but that was before the Internet. Or television. *Some of the things people wrote back in the day were so droll,* Zee thought to herself as she tried to focus but just could not... find the... moootiiivvaaa...

"Miss Carmichael?" a voice bellowed from the front of the class.

Zee shook her head. "Yes, Mrs. Pender?"

"Would you like to read the next passage? Perhaps that will help you to stay awake in our classroom today."

Zee read the passage from the old Charles Dickens novel they were studying, her interest struggling to survive with every word. Mrs. Pender, with her bifocals and her thin lips and her worn-in, dark-black Mary Janes, gave her a nod, then returned to the chalkboard. Zee started doodling in her notebook, an attempt to keep her hands busy in between writing down notes so she could stay awake for the rest of the period.

When the bell rang dismissing class, Zee moved in slow motion gathering her books and belongings into her backpack. Her mind was already onto other things, like what Izzy would bring to their study group later. Before Zee could escape the classroom, Mrs. Pender called out to her.

"Miss Carmichael, can you stay a moment?"

Zee walked over, the butterflies fluttering up in her chest.

"How are you doing, dear?" Mrs. Pender asked.

"I'm good," Zee said, "just getting adjusted to things here."

"It's a bit overwhelming, yeah?" Mrs. Pender acknowledged. "And I know you've come a long way, from the States. It's very different from your old school, right?"

"A little. But I'm ready for it," Zee said enthusiastically.

"Right, I'm sure you are. Are you getting on with your classmates okay?"

"Yes, I've met a few people, and I have a study group lined up."

"That's great," Mrs. Pender said. She looked Zee up and down and gave her a warm smile. "Listen, I know adjusting is hard, so I understand where you may be feeling tired. But try to get as much rest as possible before you come to class so you can stay alert, yeah? I've looked at your transcript and you've gotten high marks in English lit before, so I know you'll do well here if you apply yourself, mmkay?"

"Yes, Mrs. Pender, I will."

"Great," the teacher said. "I'll see you tomorrow. Get some rest."

Zee rose from her seat, suddenly more tired than she was before her talk with Mrs. Pender.

• • •

Zee was way more focused in her music theory class. Perhaps because Archie wasn't there, missing for an unknown reason. She took notes on the lecture without any distractions, read over her day's worth of schoolwork during prep, then went to play in a soccer scrimmage.

When Zee made it home, Jameela was still out at ballet practice. Zee texted Chloe with updates from her busy day before undressing out of her dirty soccer warm-ups and taking a quick shower before dinner. She dashed to the bathroom and back in less than ten minutes, long enough to miss a text from Archie.

Archie

Hey. So when can we have our own jam session? Gotta work on our performances for Festival ASAP.

Zee couldn't believe her eyes. Could it be that Archie "No New Friends" Saint John was asking her to play music with him?

Zee

Um, you want to play together?

No, he texted, then stopped typing. *I knew it,* Zee thought, her heart sinking heavily in her chest. Archie sent another message:

Archie

> I'm doing a solo piece, but I'd like your opinion on it. Thought if we could work together, you could be my inspiration. I help you, you help me.

Zee felt a warm rush to her cheeks.

Zee

> Sure, that could work.

Archie

> Great, when should we meet?

Just then, Jameela walked in the room, her hair slicked up into a tight bun. She was wearing her pink ballet tights under her navy blazer. "Evening. Are you heading to dinner?"

"Yup, just throwing on some clothes now," Zee replied in a tone that sounded as if she'd been caught licking the frosting off of the spatula.

"If you give me a few minutes to clean up, I'll walk over with you, that all right?"

Zee nodded, looking at the phone screen, biting her lower lip.

"What's going on?" Jameela asked.

"Nothing!" Zee said, nervously tossing the phone on her

bed before she could answer Archie back. "I'm starving! Let me grab my clothes. Tom is meeting us there too."

"Lovely," Jameela said in a droll tone.

• • •

Tom met the girls in the hallway by the entrance to the main dining hall. Zee was famished. Seduced by the smell of spicy meat and onions at the taco bar in the corner, she ordered up a large chicken burrito bowl, hoping that it tasted something like home. Tom grabbed a lentil burger and an iced tea. Together they walked to their table, where Jameela was already sitting with her bottle of water and a salad.

"Evening, all. How were your days?" Jameela chirped.

"All good," Tom said.

"And you, Zee?"

"Fine," she said. Jameela stared at her head, searching for more details. When she didn't get any, she answered her own question.

"Well, I had a fabulous day. I got an A on my pop quiz in algebra and I got quite a few compliments on my sewing for Skills for Life. I mean, we only had to sew the hem on a pair of jeans. But you all know how much I love fashion."

"Yes, indeed," Zee said.

"Zee, did you see your boyfriend today?"

"No, I didn't see Archie, who is not my boyfriend," Zee said quickly.

"Probably better that way. You look knackered. Maybe you should turn in early tonight."

Zee looked at Jameela. Everything was just so in its place.

Her hair. Her hands placed gently at her sides. Her perfect pleats on her perfect navy skirt on her perfect uniform. Goodness, just once a reminder that Meez Jameela was also human would be great.

"Anyway, I have to head back early because my parents are calling me from Dubai. Zee, I'll see you back at the room."

Zee threw her head back in frustration after Jameela left.

"She's a lot, yeah?" Tom said.

"A whole lot," Zee admitted.

"You know, she has issues just like the rest of us."

"You'd never know it by how she seems to float on air."

"Ha!" Tom laughed, taking a bite of his burger. "First, the ballet thing—her mom forced that on her when she was three because she wanted her to 'get some exercise and learn how to move with grace and beauty.'"

"Get out!" Zee said.

"Yeah, right? Lot of pressure for a three-year-old. Her mom is a stage mom. She pushes Jameela into these crazy dance competitions. But she is a great dancer. She even performed at the Harrods Christmas Parade a few years ago."

Zee slinked down in her seat, looking at her mismatched socks and her chewed fingernails.

"Plus, you've heard that whole thing about ballet dancers' feet. You know Jameela's have got to be a mess."

"What do you mean?" Zee asked.

"Ballet dancers have to squeeze their feet into those pointe shoes, which are super tight and super painful, leaving their feet super rough," Tom said. "All the ballerinas I know have jacked-up feet from those dreadful shoes. Jameela is so good, you know her feet have to be pretzels."

Zee sat back in her chair. She tried to create an image in her mind of Jameela taking her pointe shoes off to reveal bloody and bruised feet. But she couldn't see anything less than a raven-haired, light-as-a-feather ballerina bending her legs into an effortless plié with a perfect turnout. "C'mon, beautiful Jameela with anything less than perfect?"

Tom leaned in close to Zee. "Even a swan has duck feet."

10

JAM SESSION

Say whaaaaaaaaat?? Chloe responded after Zee texted her about her text date with Archie and her study session with Izzy. But Chloe, who had never met a celebrity she didn't like, was more interested in Izzy than Zee's new flame. *So you're going to be YouTube famous before me? Crazy! What's she like? Is she nice? Snobby? Are her friends cool? Is she smart? Does she only wear designer everything? What perfume does she wear?*

Zee looked at her phone. It was midnight in California.

She's very nice, Zee reported back. *Not snobby. Friends are normal. No, she had on H&M socks and a Topshop hairband the other day. Yes, she's very good at math. I don't know, but it smells like vanilla. More deets later. P.S.: Do you not care about my boy problems?*

Zee walked across the quad to head toward assembly. As she picked up her stride, wondering if she'd remembered all of the right notebooks for her morning classes, she heard a voice behind her say, "So, about that jam session?"

Zee inhaled quickly as Archie nudged her shoulder, fumbling to reply. "I, um, yeah, sorry I left you hanging there."

"I thought I offended you, Cali."

"No! Let's do it. What about...?"

"This afternoon. Right after class and before prep. The big concert hall. I'll bring my guitar. You bring a pen and paper and some inspiration. Don't be late."

Archie sped off ahead of Zee, who took a moment before she walked on to class, still confused about what is happening between herself and the elusive Archie Saint John.

• • •

Zee showed up a few minutes early in one of the private meeting rooms in the large concert hall building, which students often booked for practice sessions between classes. Archie was late, but that gave Zee some time to settle in, read through her journal for some song ideas, and fan herself to stop herself from sweating.

"California!" Archie announced as he walked in, carrying a guitar case in one hand, his uniform blazer in the other. "Sorry I'm late. But I've got something special for you."

Zee perked up. Did he bring a gift? Flowers? Archie saddled up close to her. "I've got... a killer song idea that I think you'll like."

Zee barely had time to get a comfortable seat before Archie took out his shiny, blonde acoustic guitar and started drumming his song. A melancholy riff came out of the guitar, followed by Archie humming.

Never finding the right thing... always looking
in the wrong place.
Never coming closer to you... drifting further, further away.
Taking time to find my way, since you and I are through.
But distance won't kill my love... my love for you.

Huh, Zee thought. A broken-hearted love song. Zee expected something more in the summer anthem genre from the jet-set rebel on campus.

Archie hummed along while he strummed his guitar, his soft-toned riffs pleasant, perhaps more pleasant without the sappy lyrics. He stopped after he sang the chorus twice and looked at Zee.

"And?"

Zee clapped in admiration. "That's great, really heartfelt."

"I compose all of my own music, usually by ear."

"Are the lyrics about someone?" Zee asked.

Archie looked at her and smiled. "No," he said. Then he turned his back and walked toward the window, humming the guitar riff.

"Oh, I just asked because the lyrics are so emotional."

"What's that mean?" Archie said. "Do I not seem like a deep kinda guy?"

"No, that's not what I mean, it's just..."

"I know what makes a great song, Zee. Whether it's about me or someone else is irrelevant. Now, you working on anything of note?"

Zee was hesitant to share her notes. Franky, her song was similar to his: she started to write about Ally, since it seemed their friendship was drifting apart. But it wasn't anywhere near finished, and she wanted to distract him so she wouldn't have to share her work quite yet.

"Where's your guitar from?" she blurted out.

"This?" Archie held the instrument out in front of him. "This is the only guitar I own that wasn't played by someone you know. I bought it off of a musician playing on the street in Monaco last summer."

"Really?" Zee said, "Some poor guy let you buy his only possession?"

"Well, he wasn't poor after the wad of cash I gave him for the guitar," Archie said. "I was walking around town and this bloke was playing off-key love songs that didn't deserve to be butchered on that lovely of a guitar. So I paid the guy double

what it was worth, and I left Monaco with a guitar. It sounds great though, perfect condition."

"Huh," Zee said.

"Right." Archie looked at his phone. "Oy, I gotta jet. Listen, I'm still working on this piece, but let's keep working together. I want to perform this at the Festival. You'll get a co-writing credit."

Zee was confused. "Co-writing? But I didn't add anything to your song. "

Archie packed up his guitar, grabbed his jacket, and walked toward the door. He turned back toward Zee before turning the knob. "Not yet. But you're, like, my muse. Muses always get credit."

He swung the door open and walked down the hallway. Zee Googled the word "muse" to triple-check she understood the word meant what she thought it meant.

Muse
(n.) MYOO-SE
person — usually a woman — who is a source of artistic inspiration

Wow, Zee thought. *This is way better than being a girlfriend.*

11

OLD FRIENDS, NEW CONNECTIONS

asper Chapman met Zee at Brookdale Academy in sixth grade when her red hair blocked his view of the chalkboard in his English class. They quickly became close friends. He had performed with Zee's band, The Beans, and threw himself into sound mixing. He'd earned quite a reputation for himself—he was the youngest person with producer credentials at Rhythm, L.A.'s biggest sound recording studio. Maybe he'd win a Grammy for sound editing before his twenty-first birthday, he liked to joke.

In the spring, before the end of seventh grade, Jasper's grandmother became ill and the family had to return to London. Jasper's parents re-enrolled him at The Hollows and told Zee's parents about the school once Mr. Carmichael accepted a new job in London. Jasper and Zee swapped notes all summer about what they'd do once they were in London.

Sadly, Jasper's grandmother passed away right at the end of summer. After the funeral Jasper returned to The Hollows after the first week of school. His teachers had been kind enough to send him the schoolwork—which included the same science and Skills for Life classes as Zee—for the first week via e-mail, which he completed at home. Now, on a crisp Saturday morning, he eagerly awaited his pals, new dorm, and old friends.

In the backseat of the Uber on the way to school, Jasper sent Zee a text: *Guess who's back in town?* Jasper wondered if she'd written any new music since they last saw each other. He missed seeing her in the last few weeks of the summer as he'd spent as much time with his grandmother as he could. During the hour-long car ride to school, Zee didn't return his text.

As Jasper rolled his bags up the two flights of stairs to his dorm room, he passed a corner single unit when he got to the top of the stairs. The name on the door said "Saint John," and he instantly knew who was inside. Archie Saint John. Resident bad boy. Wealthy know-it-all. Jasper's frenemy since year four. *Surprised he made it here before me since he's always jet-setting around,* Jasper thought.

Jasper continued down the hallway and opened the door to his room to find his roommate with his assignment for English literature next to him. A lit candle stood on his desk while he sat on the bed cross-legged, eyes focused on the flame.

"Hello, mate," the boy said without looking up.

"Hey, you must be Tom," Jasper said.

"Yes, one sec, I'm just finishing this candle-gazing exercise." *Gong!* A timer went off behind him. "Five minutes! Pretty solid for me. I do this before I get into my schoolwork. Helps me focus."

"Right," said Jasper, plopping his duffel bag onto his bed

and unzipping it. His side of the room was still tidy but barren except for a few pieces of campus mail on the desk.

"Good to see you, mate," Tom said. "Sorry about your grandmother."

"No worries. She had a good life. We got to say our goodbyes," Jasper said as he unpacked. "So have I missed anything major?"

"Nope, all is quiet on campus. Some interesting girls, some not-so-interesting schoolwork."

"Ha, right? The usual. Have you seen a girl named Zee walking around campus? Big red hair, light eyes?"

Tom looked at him and smiled. "Zeeeeeeee! She's quite the charm, yes? She's great. She's roommates with Jameela Chopra this year."

"Oh really?" Jasper perked up. "I know Zee from when I

was in L.A. We were at the same school."

"Yeah, she's finding her way around campus. We have supper most nights since she's into vegetarian food too. I also hear she might be working on some music with Archie Saint John, which is quite surprising."

"Really?" Jasper said, confused.

"That bloke is such a mystery," Tom said. "Never makes time for anyone, but likes the new girl from California? I don't get it."

"That chap," said Jasper, shaking his head. "I'm shocked he's even in school right now. Didn't he only go to about three weeks' worth of classes last year? How did the school chancellor even pass him to the next level?"

"Donations from his parents, that's why."

"Right. Anyway, lunch must be soon, right? I texted Zee a little bit ago, but she still hasn't texted me back. Strange. Maybe you can text her and see if she's joining for lunch? I can show up as a surprise.'"

Tom sent the text message to Zee, and casually tossed his phone on his bed. He blew out the candle he used for his meditation and got himself ready, brushing his hair in the mirror. Jasper was surprised Zee hadn't answered him yet. Maybe she's busy. With her studying. Or something. Or someone.

"Are you putting on your uniform for lunch or just going to scrub it out?"

Jasper looked at his white T-shirt that was slightly damp from unpacking and arranging his room. His blue jeans had a chocolate stain from this morning's bowl of cereal. "Right. I'll clean up and be ready in a bit."

· · ·

The main dining hall was abuzz for a Saturday, fully packed with hungry students. Izzy strolled into the cafeteria with two friends, one filing from behind carrying her phone in landscape position, the other in fast-paced conversation with Izzy on camera. Izzy gave a wave as she marched by Zee and Jameela, who were waiting for Tom. He had mentioned that he had a surprise for us when we got here.

Jameela surveyed the lunch offerings but opted for a simple tomato soup and a slice of toast with a schmear of peanut butter. "That's all?" Zee asked.

"My stomach is a bit shaky," Jameela said.

Zee ordered a turkey shepherd's pie and a lemon bar, and pushed her tray down the counter. But before she could grab her ID card, a familiar voice called out toward her.

"Do they have shepherd's pies in California?" Jasper asked.

Zee turned around in slight disbelief and hugged her friend tightly. "*Ohmylanta*, hiiii! How are you? When did you get back?"

"Today. I texted you on the way. Didn't you get it?"

Zee looked down at her phone to check the text messages, but then thought twice of it, afraid that Jasper might see the barrages of texts between her and Archie.

"I must have had my phone tucked away," Zee said. "Well, I'm glad you're here now."

Jasper's black eyes were fixed on Zee. "I'm rooming with Tom, and I know you all get on well."

"Yes! We're meeting him for lunch. Is he with you?" Zee said. "Oh, wait, you're the surprise!"

"He grabbed our table for us so we can all sit together. It's so good to see you!"

"Yeah," Zee said. "You as well. Grab your food and I'll meet you at the table."

"All right," Jasper replied. He piled a few slices of roasted chicken, potatoes, and a cookie on his plate, grabbed a glass of milk, and headed over to the table where Tom, Jameela, and Zee were already huddled.

"So really, what have I missed?" Jasper asked as he sat down next to Tom, across from Zee.

"Nothing really, just getting adjusted to school. I have circuitry in science class this term and it's really tough."

"Oh, I can help you with that, Zee," Jasper said.

"Yeah, I could use it!"

"You want to study together? We could meet at the library after class."

Zee took a bite of her lunch. "That'd be great, but I already have a study thing going with Izzy Matthews."

Jasper looked surprised. "Izzy Matthews, YouTube star? You're studying with her?"

"Yeah, she's really great at algebra. You want to join our study group?"

Jasper had assumed Zee would be his study partner for most classes given their friendship. But Zee told him that she and Izzy already had two successful study sessions for their English and algebra classes, and Zee had scored above-average marks on pop quizzes for both classes. "Mrs. Pender even said I did nice work in front of the class," Zee said.

"I mean, I don't know Izzy that well," Jasper said. "I've just seen her around campus."

"Oh, she's super cool. I can ask her if it's okay."

Jasper went back to his lunch, looking at Zee from the corner of his eye. Something seemed different about his friend. He couldn't describe it, but he sure felt it.

"Hey, Zee, I have to have you listen to this new track I'm working on. It's wicked. I think if Brookdale had a theme song, this is what it would be. I might do it for the Festival. I'm not sure."

Zee looked up at Jasper. "Cool! Yeah, I started working with Archie on his Festival song too."

Jasper blinked and shook his head. Tom and Jameela looked at each other, then looked at Zee.

"You *what* with Archie? Archie Saint John?"

"Yeah. Well, we have music theory together, and he knows I write songs..."

"How does he know that?"

"Because I told him when I saw him at lunch on the first day of school," Zee said, scrunching her face. "Anyway, he shared a piece he was working on with me the other day and I gave him some feedback."

"Shared where?" Jasper asked. Jameela leaned in to hear the conversation better. She hadn't heard much about that jam session from Zee and seemed eager for details.

"We met at the concert hall. What's with the third degree?"

Jasper clenched his teeth. Archie was the type of guy who took what he needed from people and moved on. Was he preying on his friend to have her do his schoolwork? This whole thing sounded too innocent to be true.

"But Zee," Jasper started. Then he stopped. Maybe he was overreacting. It was just the first week of school. "Nothing,

I just... I guess I'm just surprised. Archie usually keeps to himself."

"I gathered that from both Jameela's warnings and the tone of the song he played me," Zee said. "But he is talented."

"I don't doubt it," Jasper said. "Well, maybe you can make some time to listen to my song. I've always valued your opinion on my work. What are you doing for the rest of the day?"

Zee had no Saturday plans except for one important phone call in the afternoon. "I dunno," she replied.

"Why don't we go to the main town square today and check it out? We could grab a tea there, and we'll be back way before curfew."

"Sure, sounds great," said Zee. "I haven't been off campus yet. Let's meet at the arch at the entryway."

"Does anybody else want to come?" Jasper asked.

"I've got to go to ballet practice," Jameela said.

"I might want to go grab some more tea at the health food place on Main Street," Tom said.

"Cool, see you in like an hour or so?" Zee said. "Let's go before four. I have to be back for a meeting."

• • •

Tom, Jasper, and Zee met at the big arch at the main entrance of the campus and walked toward the town's main square. Main Street was a row of boutiques and historic centers that included the main campus bookstore, a family-owned health food store, the chemist, and the coffee shop where Archie saw The Scene the other night. Older residents, families with strollers and baby carriers, and The Hollows students all flocked to the area on the weekends to shop, eat, gather, and enjoy the crisp fall air. Zee and her friends talked eagerly about school, where they could find chocolate-covered almonds, and which of these shops sold green tea for Tom and a blueberry muffin for Zee.

Jasper played his new song off of his cell phone as they walked. "I like, I like," Zee said excitedly, bobbing her head to the upbeat tune. She took his phone to hold the speaker closer to her ear. She was so lost in the music that she didn't notice when Tom and Jasper trotted across the street ahead of her.

Zee looked up and tried to catch up to her friends, but when she stepped her foot out onto the crosswalk, a loud honking horn interrupted her dance party to Jasper's beats.

"Crikey!" said the voice behind the midsized sedan that almost smacked into Zee's right leg. "Watch where you're going!"

"Sorry!" she yelled, scurrying across the street on shaky legs, her heart beating in her chest.

Tom and Jasper turned back around at the commotion and waited for their friend. "You forget cars drive on the other side of the road here?" Jasper said.

"That's going to take forever to remember," Zee said.

The three turned the corner onto Main Street and passed the local hardware store. "Don't you need some mounting hooks for that sound-mixing equipment in the room?" Tom asked.

"Good idea," Jasper said. While they went inside, Zee went to the pharmacy to pick up some personal items—tooth floss, deodorant, body wash. Girl stuff. Stuff she didn't want the boys to see her buying.

They regrouped and headed toward the health food store for Tom's green tea, and then to the bookstore. Jasper needed a few more books for class and this was the first time he'd been able to get to the campus shop.

Finally, they hit Moe's Coffee Shop, a neighborhood fixture since the '80s. Inside, Izzy and her roommate, Poppy, were sitting at a front table by the window coffee shop. Zee waved hello to Izzy as she walked by.

"Hi, Zee!" Izzy called out. "What's up?"

"Hi, Izzy! All good!"

Izzy got up from her seat and walked over to the three of them. She gave Zee a one-armed hug, and nodded at Tom, who asked what they all wanted to order. Izzy passed on a drink—"I've got a latte at the table"—then pivoted to look Jasper in the eye. Jasper recalled Izzy from her videos but really hadn't talked to her much before. "I know we've shared a bunch of classes. I'm Izzy."

"Jasper. Hi," he said politely. "I've seen you on campus. And YouTube."

"Yes, ha! Nicer to connect in person. What are you all up to?"

"Ordering iced tea for the moment," Zee said. "And then back to campus. Oh, Jasper has circuitry with me and he's amazing at computers and stuff. I told him we get together to study during the week and thought he could join us. He'll basically teach us to be engineers, he's that good."

Izzy's blue eyes widened and her teeth sparkled as she talked. "That would be great!"

Jasper smiled shyly. "I can't make any guarantees, but yes, I do know my way around a circuit board. Where do you all meet?"

"At prep. We take a table in the back so I can film there," Izzy said, stepping closer to Jasper.

"Sounds great. I'll be there after I drop my stuff off from music classes and pick up my science books."

Izzy nodded in approval. "Awesome. Happy to have you. It will be nice to have a different perspective in the group as well."

Jasper ran his fingers through his hair and turned back toward the menu above the register. Izzy continued looking at the back of his head until she seemed to remember Zee was still standing next to her.

"Oh, also, Zeeeee," Izzy sang. "What are you doing next weekend? We're having a sleepover at my house. I'd love for you to come."

Zee's eyes jumped open. "Absolutely!"

"Great! We'll meet after classes Friday. My dad will pick us up from the dorms at 4 p.m. I'm excited to show you around. You haven't spent much time off campus, right?"

"No, I haven't," said Zee. "Except for today's outing for snacks and body wash."

"We'll have fun!" Izzy said before leaving. "And bring your bathing suit."

She has a pool? Zee wondered.

"Yes, she has a pool," Tom said. "And yes, that means what you think it means."

12

THE ZEE FILES

*B*etween school, after-school activities, and the time difference, Zee, Ally, and Chloe found it hard to stay in touch. After a dozen missed calls, texts, DMs, and IMs, the three decided to schedule a video chat the weekend. The only time that worked for all of them was Saturday at 4:15 p.m., London time.

"Hi!" Zee said when the virtual room opened up. Chloe was already on the call wearing a Brookdale Academy T-shirt and oversized black-framed glasses. "It's been FOR-EV-AH!"

"I knoooowwww!" said Chloe. "Okay, it's been a week."

"Still," said Zee. Ally logged in shortly after, waving at the group as she sipped a beverage from a dainty porcelain mug.

"Has it been that long?" said a more subdued Ally. "Zee, didn't I just talk to you the other day?"

"About homework!" Zee replied. "Not about the important stuff! Chlo, did you get a haircut?"

"No, it's just pulled away from my face. I've been rocking it up in a bun with soccer and stuff since school started."

"How is Brookdale this year?" Ally asked.

"It's still Brookdale," Chloe reported. "Everything is pretty. The teachers are all there. Oh, remember our old counselor Mr. Brown? He retired. Oh, and our cafeteria now serves kombucha slushies. I have one, like, every day."

"Mmmm, so good." Zee said.

"Ally, how's Paris?" Chloe asked.

"Fine," Ally said, keeping it brief. "*C'est la vie.*"

"Say la who?" Zee asked.

"It's a saying, Zee, like 'such is life.' As in, things are what they are and they're fine."

Zee scrunched her face. "Okaaay, well, can I tell you what happened to me this week? I think I went on a virtual date!"

Chloe and Ally's faces jumped with surprise on their respective screens. "With who?"

"This guy named Archie. He's like the hottest guy in the class."

"Where did you go?"

"Nowhere. Well, he was out watching this band at a coffee shop while I was in my room. We texted the entire show."

"What did he say in the texts?" Ally asked, looking down at something on her desk.

"It was mostly about the band, but we talked—or texted—for like two hours. And he asked me to listen to some of his own music."

"Send us a picture!" Chloe said.

Zee grabbed her phone and looked for his profile on the school intranet, the same directory where Archie found Zee's e-mail address. "Hold on, I'm looking," Zee said. "Ah, there he is!" She held up his photo to the screen of her computer camera. "Can you guys see?"

"Sort of," Chloe said. "Yeah. Wow. WOW. Okay! You had pillow talk with this guy?"

"About music, Chlo," Zee responded.

"Sweet music, I'm sure."

"Anyway!" Zee said, blushing.

Ally came back into focus. "Hey guys, I'm sorry but I have to head out. My mom is coming for dinner and I have to pack and get ready."

"You have to pack for dinner?" Zee asked. "Goodness, I thought we'd have more time. I also thought it would be easier for us to link up."

"But we're all on all the platforms," Chloe said. "We're still in contact."

"The time difference is so hard to manage," Zee said.

"When it's morning here, Chloe's sleeping, and by the time you get home from school, Ally and I are already asleep."

Chloe nodded. "Truth. So should we have a standing conference call date on Saturdays at 4:15 p.m. so we can at least chat in person?"

"That's a start," Ally called over her shoulder, already moving about her room to get ready for dinner.

"Yes," Zee said. "But I also feel like we are chasing each other on too many platforms. What if we create our own system? Like our own internal file system where we can drop whatever we like in the file and we'll get notifications when someone adds something new so we know to check in. And this way all of our pictures, audio files, video, homework, songs, artwork, news clips, and stuff can all live in one place."

"That sounds good," Chloe said. "But what if I really need to talk to you?"

"Look, we can always text or call each other," Zee said. "But like with the Archie thing—I've got text messages here I want to show you, plus music clips and his photo. That's a lot to try and message to someone, especially if you're asleep and I know you won't see it. With our folder, I can assemble everything into one file, like a virtual scrapbook. And everyone can see it at once."

"And we can clear it out every week so everything can stay super secret," said Chloe.

"Yes!" said Zee.

"The Files," said Chloe. "The *Zee* Files."

"That's catchy," Ally said. "I'll look out for it when you create the folder. Bye, girls!"

"Bye, Ally!" said Chloe. "Zee, make sure to put that photo of

Archie in the file. You know, for reference. Later!"

Zee smiled. The Zee Files. A private communications platform. Secure, convenient, open 24-7. Zee created an online file on her computer, then added Ally and Chloe as co-authors. She marked it private and dropped a photo of Archie and a few of the music clips that he had sent her via text message. She included comments: *I fell asleep to this song. He sang the chorus to me. At least I think he did, I can't remember. Because I fell asleep. LOL.*

Zee closed the file on her computer and labeled it "The Zee Files" on the desktop. Then she logged off of the conference call and pushed herself away from her desk, happy to be in closer contact with her two best friends and pleased with how she problem solved their need to communicate better.

If I can launch a personal file-sharing platform, surely I can get through circuitry class, Zee thought.

13

LATE NIGHTS

Izzy, her roommate, Poppy, and their friend CJ held court at their regular back table in the large study hall for prep. Their books were out and open with colorful notes written in multicolored pens. Izzy's classic cursive writing could have been printed on greeting cards.

"Hi hi!" Zee greeted as she approached the table. "Have you all started going over algebra yet?"

Izzy, taking a sip of water from her water bottle, waved as Zee sat down. "Not yet, we're just getting started."

Zee opened her bag and took out her books just as Jasper glided into the room and found the girls. Izzy immediately perked up when he approached the table.

"Hiiiiii! We've been waiting for you," Izzy said. "Maybe we should start with science first since we have Jasper here."

Zee's eyebrows arched upward. "Okay, sure. But we have another quiz in algebra coming up. Are you guys going to study for it?"

"Yeah, we'll get to it, but let's lead with Jasper's favorite subject since he's new to the group."

Jasper sat down next to Zee. "Aww, that's very kind, Izzy. Shame we're not meeting in a kitchen. We could have cooked up something proper for our culinary homework."

"Maybe next time?" Izzy said. "Ooh, that could make for a fun video. I could do a Cook with Me vlog! And we can all be in it! Jasper, what's your favorite thing to make?"

"A mess," Zee joked. "Remember that time we made a cake for Chloe's birthday and we had more flour on the floor than we did in the cake?"

"Yeah, your mom ended up saving that cake in the end. It was still good though."

"Chloe ate three pieces!" Zee laughed.

The crew opened their circuitry notes and Izzy leaned in close to Jasper as he talked through the day's lesson, a primer on how a camera worked. "It's amazing that even the most basic of cameras can take the most amazing pictures," Jasper said.

"Yeah," Izzy said. "Oh, speaking of cameras... smile, Jasper, let's get you on camera and introduce everyone to my vlog. Say 'heyyyyyyy!'"

"Oh, wait, I don't need to be introduced, I'm not..."

"Yes, you are! You're our newest star here," Izzy prodded. "C'mon!"

"No, I really don't have to..."

"Tell everyone your naaaaaammmeeee," Izzy prodded while Poppy and CJ giggled.

Jasper looked away shyly, then flashed his sparkling smile and waved his hand. "Hello, hi, I'm Jasper."

Zee flipped open her science notebook, giving Izzy a

sideways glance. *She's really gushing up to Jasper,* she thought. *I don't think I've seen anyone so excited about studying ever.*

Izzy pointed the camera to Zee. "And this is Zeeee, who you all saw in the last video. She and Jasper were buddies back in California."

Zee gave a bashful smile to the camera. She suddenly felt like a third wheel between Izzy and Jasper, as if Izzy had forgotten all about her homework once Jasper arrived, though Jasper was there to help them get a better grasp of their studies. Maybe she was reading into it too much, but it seemed Izzy had a crush on Jasper.

"Right, so like, the *science*," Izzy said. "We're here for the science, right?"

"Right, right," Jasper said. "Do you have your notes from today's session?"

Izzy kept the camera pointed on Jasper, smiling behind it, as Jasper continued explaining the circuitry lessons from the last few days. Zee tried to follow along, but it became too difficult between Izzy's giggling and interrupting with side conversations. Finally, Zee grew tired of the banter.

"Guys, I'm going to head back before dinner and clean up. See you tomorrow in class."

Zee gathered her books and belongings and walked out of the study hall, leaving Jasper and Izzy to giggle on camera without her.

• • •

Jameela's clothes and sheets hardly ever need to be washed, Zee noted as she rose out of bed. Her sheets were perfectly made each morning when Zee woke up, and two nights ago Jameela didn't come back to bed until twenty minutes before lights out, missing curfew by more than an hour. Most of the girls in the dorm at least gathered to watch reruns of *The Great British Bake Off* an hour before heading to bed. But Jameela was never around.

Then Wednesday night happened.

Zee had a busy day of classes, a yoga class for her after-school sports hour, and study group with Izzy and Jasper. Jameela didn't go to dinner with Zee and the gang, and she

still hadn't returned to the room when the dorm advisor came around looking for her. "I haven't seen her since earlier in the day," Zee told the advisor, but she secretly worried where her roommate could be. Finally, Zee texted Jameela.

Zee

> **Hey, the authorities are out looking for you.**

No response.
Zee waited twenty minutes, then tried her again.

Zee

> **Hey, like, I'm worried. Are you okay?**

No response again.

Zee changed into her pajamas. Her lips pursed as she brushed her hair and wrapped it up in the vintage silk scarf her mom gave her. Just as she slid into bed with her journal, a key jiggled in the doorknob and Jameela appeared.

"Hello, sorry I'm late. Just working on my Festival piece."

"Dorm advisor was looking for you."

"I know, I told her why I was late. It's okay."

Zee looked puzzled. "You were working on your piece... at the studio?"

"Oh no, they close the dance studios after dinner. I was, um, someplace else."

"Someplace else?" Zee turned her legs so that she faced Jameela. "You've missed curfew twice, and every time you do the dorm advisor comes looking. What do I say the next time you're not around?"

"Say that I'm dancing."

"Is that what you're really doing?"

"What do you think I'm doing? Of course I'm dancing. Ballet is not easy, you know. After a full day of sitting in classes, it takes me an hour just to warm up enough to be able to point my toes."

"I'm sure," Zee said, perplexed. "I was just concerned."

"Great," Jameela said, "and now, I'm exhausted." She quickly slipped into her pajamas and went to bed.

• • •

Despite two study group sessions with Jasper and Izzy, Zee still couldn't grasp circuitry. Zee was thirsty for Jasper's knowledge on the subject. But Izzy had little interest in studying and she spent more time filming herself goofing around with Jasper than going over notes.

In science class, Zee's head rested heavily in the palm of her hand as she drifted out of consciousness. The teacher, Mr. Roth, paced slowly back and forth in front of the blackboard and introduced each concept with a block-lettered word written on the chalkboard.

A few minutes before the end of class, Mr. Roth handed back the pop quizzes they took the day before. He placed a piece of paper face down on Zee's desk. "Miss Carmichael, you might want to take better notes for the quiz next week," Mr. Roth said. Zee winced as she moved her fingers slowly to the edge of the paper. A red "34" was written on the paper. As in, thirty-four percent of the questions were answered correctly. A failing grade.

"Oh. My. Lanta," Zee said. Her heart raced. Her palms grew super sweaty, and she wondered if she needed to drop out of Izzy's study group before she flunked out of school.

· · ·

The next day, Zee called her mother while she packed her bag for her trip to Izzy's house.

"I can't believe you're going to someone else's home before coming home to see us," said Mrs. Carmichael.

"I know, but Izzy invited me and I didn't want to be rude," Zee said. "Besides, you said you were remodeling the kitchen. I don't want to sleep in a construction zone."

"Well, your room is still untouched. Except for the bed."

"What? What happened to my bed?"

"I told you I was going to buy another one. I put your old one in the spare bedroom."

"I love that bed!" Zee said, letting out a groan. "Guess I'll sleep in the spare bedroom when I come home."

"Darling, no. The rest of your room is exactly as you left it. How's school going? Good?"

"Yeah it's fine," Zee said, omitting the details about her struggles with her schoolwork. "I finally caught up with Jasper too."

"Oh good! Is he doing all right after the funeral?"

"Yeah, he seems great as always. He joined my study group with Izzy, so we're all studying together." Zee's mind drifted back to the study group the day before and how Izzy was so eager to be around Jasper. Did she have a crush on him? And if so, why did that make Zee grit her teeth? "Well, I gotta finish packing. I'll be back on Sunday. And you can also text me if you need me."

"I'll let you have fun with your friends. Izzy is quite popular on YouTube, right?" Mrs. Carmichael asked. "Maybe you can get her to link to me and we can do a follow-for-follow or something. Boost each other's following!"

Zee rolled her eyes. "Mom, I don't think it works that way, but yeah, maybe."

14

GIRLS' NIGHT OUT

*I*zzy's father picked up the girls in a black Range Rover. Izzy, sitting in the front seat, quickly turned up the volume on the stereo and started playing her "Road Trippin'" playlist from her phone. She lip-synced along to the songs while she filmed herself, then turned the camera on Poppy and Zee in the backseat to get footage of her "backup singers." Zee giggled, but inside, she wondered when would be the right time to bring up to Izzy that their unproductive study groups led to her failing the last quiz.

Their road trip was just thirty minutes away, as Izzy's family lived in Gloucestershire in the Cotswolds on an expansive estate with twenty-three acres of land. Zee's eyes took in the leafy England countryside as they drove to the family property. A long driveway rolled in between tall evergreens, lush gardens, and horse stables. The drive opened up to a large family home that looked like something out of a mid-century fairy tale.

"Welcome, girls," Mr. Matthews said as they pulled up to

the house. Zee had not been in a home this large since Chloe took her to the Malibu mansion of one of her dad's clients who had won a few Grammys and just finished the soundtrack for a big-budget Hollywood action film. Zee got out of the car, her mouth floating open as her eyes followed the ivy growing up the side of the large home, which in her mind would hereby be classified as an English manor.

Izzy had her phone out to record reactions upon arriving home. The English spaniels Izzy had in one of her earlier YouTube videos greeted her with wet noses and wagging tails. "Hi guys! Oh, look at you two! That's Kingston on the right, and that's Baron over there," Izzy said, introducing the dogs to her guests.

Izzy led her friends up the walkway to the large wooden door of her house. "We've had this home in our family for nine generations. It goes back to the 1700s," she explained.

The girls meandered through the door into the front great room, with its tufted leather furniture and classic novels on the bookshelves, and framed pictures of family members past and present. They walked down a dimly lit hallway lined with paintings and photographs, and two doors opened up to the second large room. Next to it was a modern kitchen with sleek, stainless-steel appliances, white sleek cabinets, and a large glass ceiling. Past the kitchen island, a patio in the back of the house opened to a pool and a path leading to the rest of the grounds, which Izzy told them included a tennis court, gardens, and a smaller carriage house for guests. Mrs. Matthews, who had short blonde hair and blue eyes, came out of the opposite entrance to the kitchen to greet the girls.

"Hello, hello," she said politely. "Izzy, their rooms are ready.

Do you girls want some tea or something to eat?"

"Please, that sounds lovely," Izzy replied.

Zee took in the huge house with her mouth agape. "How do you not get lost in this place?"

"It's not that big! We primarily hang out in the kitchen and around the patio during the summer. C'mon, let me show you your rooms."

Zee's eyes widened. "We each get our own room?"

"There are three rooms next to mine that are usually empty. So you guys can choose from those."

"It's like you have your own wing of the house," Zee said, awed.

The girls wandered up a staircase from the kitchen and landed in a den with a large flat-screen television and a comfortable-looking sofa. From there, a long, banister-lined

hallway ran along four doors. The first was Izzy's room, which contained a four-poster bed draped with fluffy, white plush bedding, a stack of pillows, and a foot bench. The room was painted millennial pink and the furniture had gold accents. On the walls hung framed photographs, some of which were taken at the beach, others in the woods or in what looked like Izzy's backyard. Izzy was in a few of them, but most of them were of other people. A desk sat under a large window opposite the bed, complete with a lamp and printer.

Izzy jumped on the bed and fanned her arms up overhead and then back down, like she was making a snow angel in the comforter. "Ahhhh, I've missed you."

Zee's eyes traveled along the wall and she saw Izzy's camera. "Your photographs are really great."

"Thanks! It's all about having great subjects," Izzy said. "Let's keep going. I'll show you each to your rooms."

The three additional rooms, small but neatly decorated, were made up similarly to each other. Each had a queen-size bed with a desk, large closet, nightstands with lamps, and large mirrors opposite the closet. A window facing south overlooked the back of the grounds. "I can take this one," Zee said when Izzy pointed to the first guest room.

"We might not even sleep in the beds. Remember last time we were here we passed out on the couch during a movie?" said Izzy.

"Yes!" Poppy said. "What was the name of that god-awful flick again?"

"I can't remember. Something about a woman and a job at a magazine and she lived in this ridiculous apartment in New York City. And she was getting married, but then called it off.

I don't know. Anyway, Pops, did you bring the tripod from the room?"

Izzy ran behind her friends with her phone. She filmed their interactions while the girls unpacked and played around with makeup in the bathroom, went up and down the halls and in and out of each other's rooms, tried on each other's clothes, and gossiped about school. School. When Zee thought about school she felt the anxiety of having to improve her grades, but when Izzy and her pals talked about it they discussed it like they were scouting scenes for a movie. "Should we ask Mrs. Templeton if we can film in the kitchen next week for that Cook with Me shoot? Oh, Zee! Pick out a recipe for it and we'll make it together!" Izzy's enthusiasm to include her in filming made Zee forget temporarily about her bombed circuitry quiz.

Zee smiled as she unzipped her bag in her room, looking around at the space. She heard giggles from the bathroom and had a flashback of hanging out with Chloe and Ally together in California. She wondered what they were up to today on this beautiful Saturday afternoon. Zee took a photo of her room and the view from her window, and uploaded the photo to the Zee Files for Chloe and Ally. *Guest digs at Izzy's,* Zee wrote. *Better than Soho House.*

"You guys want to go swimming? The pool's heated," Izzy announced.

The girls changed into swimsuits and headed to the patio, where lemonades and iced teas, sliced fruits, and popsicles were arranged on a table for them to snack on by the pool. Zee took a photo of the snack spread, uploaded it to the Zee Files, tossed her phone on a lounger, and dove into the pool.

···

Izzy's family had a chef, a middle-aged, trim man with dark hair and a wide smile. For dinner, he cooked for the girls a variety of Mediterranean-style dinner with kabobs and fresh salads, and also made a four-course dinner for Izzy's parents who were hosting friends in another part of the home. The amount of food going in and out of the kitchen, carried by both the chef and two house managers, was enough to feed Zee's entire school dorm. "Do you guys compost?" Zee asked the chef after noticing how many dirty dishes accumulated after the meals.

"No, but a lot of the edible food scraps do end up going to the horses," the chef replied.

After dinner, the girls made s'mores over a firepit on the patio, and the chef brought out individual servings of sticky toffee puddings while they laughed and watched the stars poke through the darkening sky. Afterward, they came inside, changed into their pajamas, and settled in for a movie. In the second-floor den next to the bedrooms, they found large bowls of popcorn laid out on cozy blankets, with slippers in front of each blanket and bowl setup. "Hot chocolate, tea, seltzer water?" a woman who Izzy said was the house manager asked each girl.

"This feels like home," Zee said to Izzy. "Thank you so much for inviting me."

"Of course, Zee! Welcome to The Hollows." Izzy held up a mug of hot chocolate, and the two other girls clanked their mugs with hers.

"Most of us know each other from other boarding schools or primary school or something, so it must be a bit hard to come in from another country," Izzy said after she took a sip of her hot chocolate. "But you have Jasper, and he's *lovely*."

"Yes, he's great."

"And I see you've become friendly with Archie, which is a miracle. He doesn't hang out with anyone, you know."

"Yeah, I've heard. I guess we just share a passion for music and that's what bonds us."

"Perhaps. Or perhaps he really, really fancies you."

"Fancy me? Oh goodness," Zee said. "I would think Jameela is more his type."

"Jameela? No way. Plus, Jameela is so focused on that ballet she hardly has time for anything else."

Zee asked curiously, "How long have you known Jameela?"

"I met her last year in the dorms. She was much happier then. Optimistic, smiling all the time. But then something changed. I think she's having a hard time adapting to... changes."

"Like what?"

"Well, last year she was smaller. This year she's matured. Like, her body's grown. Which can't be good for ballet. I heard a rumor that her ballet teacher said something to her about being too curvy, and since then she's been trying to lose weight and work extra hard to prove the teacher wrong."

"Huh," Zee said, nodding. "That could explain why she doesn't eat much."

"And also explain her mood this year. She's downright sullen. It's hard to be happy when you're hungry and insecure."

Zee stared into her popcorn as a British romcom blared over the television. It all made sense, Zee thought. Those late nights coming home in her ballet leotard. The dinners of lettuce and peanuts and nothing more. And Jameela's curtness toward her.

Halfway through the film Zee's head leaned off to one side, and she fell asleep with one hand in her popcorn. Eventually, all the girls all fell asleep around the television. As the credits rolled, Poppy crept away to her room. Soon after, Izzy nudged Zee good night as she walked to her room, smiling down at her. Zee shook herself awake long enough to remove her hand out of her popcorn bowl, tiptoe to her room, and flop into bed.

• • •

The next morning, the girls woke up to the smell of sizzling eggs and pancakes in the kitchen. Izzy was already awake, helping the chef and her mother arrange a breakfast bar of fresh loaves of bread, fruits, jams, granola, and a selection of herbal teas to go along with scrambled eggs and buckwheat pancakes. "Morning! Did you all sleep well?" Mrs. Matthews greeted. The girls nodded, their eyes growing wide at the smorgasbord of yummy goodies in front of them.

After breakfast, the girls headed into town to do some shopping, popping into the town square's shops and boutiques. One shop sold artisanal honey, and another sold stylish women's clothing. "I got my pajamas here," Izzy said, nodding to the store. "Let's go in." Izzy filmed everything, even the cashier ringing up the fifty pounds' worth of hair accessories Izzy bought for school.

After a day of shopping, Izzy's dad drove the girls back to campus. They arrived early enough in the evening to allow the girls time to settle back into campus before the week began and for Izzy to edit the video from her weekend and post on YouTube before she went to bed. Zee returned to her empty room. Jameela was likely off at dance practice. Zee unpacked her suitcase and contemplated a shower, then planned to upload photos and a message to Ally and Chloe in the Zee Files before she went to bed.

As Zee grabbed her robe, her phone started buzzing. A notification for a text message from Archie popped up on the screen.

Archie

> How goes it, Cali? Studying for that music theory quiz we have tomorrow?

Zee texted back, *Hello, and yeah.* Zee had already reviewed the notes before leaving for Izzy's house, but she lied because she didn't feel like telling him she had to study algebra and science tonight. She didn't share either of those classes with Archie.

Archie responded, *Great, me too. Wanna study together?*

Zee didn't sleep that well at Izzy's the night before. Despite 500-thread-count sheets and a foam mattress that curved around every inch of her body, Zee never slept that well outside of her own bed. She planned to take the night to study in her pajamas and headscarf, in the privacy of her own room. Zee didn't feel like getting dressed and putting on lip gloss, not even for Archie.

I'm worn out from the weekend. Catch up tomorrow? she texted back. She wondered if she was sounding more English by the day.

A two-minute pause went by. And then a simple emoji of a guy with a flat expression.

I'll see you first thing, I promise, Zee responded, trying to sound somewhat enthused.

Don't leave me hanging again, Cali?

Yes, sure, Zee wrote.

She took an exasperated breath as she tossed her phone on her bed. Then she turned on her computer and opened up the Zee Files to check for new updates from Izzy and Chloe. Zee loaded a few pictures from this weekend and some notes.

Izzy's house is just like you see on the YouTube video, except with more staff. It's crazy. Her parents are just as nice as she is. I also ate my weight in sticky toffee pudding. That stuff might be my favorite thing about England. #yumyumyum

Zee also filled the girls in on Jameela, worried about what was happening with her. *Why do I care so much?* Zee wondered. Maybe because it was hard to ignore, given that Jameela slept just five feet from her. Zee didn't have the physical or mental space to allow more drama to upset her already unsettled mind.

Then she noticed there was a new note from Chloe in

the Zee Files. Chloe had uploaded the latest edition of *The Brookdale Beat*, Brookdale Academy's school newspaper, which she edited. There was an article in the sports page about the soccer team—which Chloe was an outfielder for—but also a great "Where Are They Now" story about the members of The Beans that Chloe wrote. *So fun! I had no idea you were writing that!* Zee typed back in a comment.

Ally left a short response to both Zee and Chloe's notes, but didn't leave anything about herself in the file. Zee texted Ally to see if she happened to be around.

Zee

Hello?

Ally

Hey.

Zee

Heeeyyy! Whatcha doing?.

Ally

On my way to eat with Dad.

Zee

Ah, got it. I just put a bunch of stuff in the Zee Files. Jameela's been missing curfew. I just can't believe it. I don't think she knows, but I am, like, scared for her. And I'm struggling in math and science, which I thought Jasper could help me with, but he's preoccupied by Izzy.

Ally didn't respond.

Zee

Hey, you there?

Ally

Things are fine. Busy. Can we talk later?

Zee

Sure.

Zee rolled her eyes. *Every time I reach out, it's as if I'm interrupting something,* Zee thought.

Zee pulled out her circuitry notes and tried to focus, but now she was worried that something was up with Ally too. Ally. Jameela. Circuitry. Archie. Zee's eyes crossed as if the circuitry in her own preoccupied mind was about to overload.

15

THE MISSING BALLERINA

Tom! I don't know where Jameela is.

Zee stopped typing. This deserved a phone call. She frantically dialed Tom since he knew her roommate the longest of their friends. Zee asked him if there may be a chance he had her parents' cell phone number in case they couldn't reach her.

"What do you mean?"

"I mean she didn't come home at all last night. Not even back to the room to sleep. Her sheets are exactly as she left them the day before. Everything is still like the day before. Her eye mask is in the same spot, her purse, everything."

"Well, where could she be? And how did she not get stopped by the headmaster or dorm advisor?".

"I don't know!" Zee said. "All I know is it's 6:45 a.m and my roommate did not sleep here last night. I have no idea if she's dead or alive!"

"Hold on, drama queen," Tom said. "She's probably alive and just oversleeping in some dark corner of a dance studio somewhere. Did you text her?"

"Twelve times. Just in the last twenty minutes."

"Okay, I wouldn't text you back either. You're not her mother."

"I know, but..."

"She'll be fine. Let's meet up during the morning break. If she's not back before we go to classes, then we'll call security. Sound good?"

Zee rolled her eyes, but agreed.

After getting dressed and gathering her long, curly hair into a high bun, Zee loaded up her backpack with her books and notes. She stuffed her phone in her jacket pocket, keeping it on in case Jameela called. *This is so unlike her*, Zee thought. *But like Tom said, I'm not Jameela's mother.*

Zee stepped out into the hallway, locking the door behind her. She was deep in thought as she walked down the hallway and turned the corner when Jameela, at 7:28 a.m., almost twelve hours past curfew, turned the same corner wearing a leotard under her school jacket. She looked up at Zee. Dark circles settled in under her eyes and her high bun had strays floating around her head like jellyfish tentacles.

"Jameela," Zee greeted, surprised at her roommate's fatigued appearance. "Are you okay? I was worried when I woke up and you weren't in bed."

"I'm fine," Jameela said, holding her chin up intentionally. "I fell asleep in the common room downstairs."

Zee was puzzled. If that were the case, shouldn't a dorm advisor or some adult have seen her? "You fell asleep in a common space and no one woke you up? Or took you back to our room?"

Jameela's cheeks grew hot as she began walking toward their room. "Yes. Amazing, huh?"

Zee followed quickly behind her. "Amazing. Unbelievable, really."

Jameela yawned, then looked at Zee with her lips pursed. She turned the doorknob and flung herself into the room. "Are you calling me a liar?"

"No!" Zee said, following her inside. "But something's up with you. You're never here, you're not coming home in time for curfew, and now you're not coming home at all?"

"So sorry I didn't check in, warden."

"I'm not the one who's breaking all the rules here, so why are you treating me like the criminal?"

Jameela threw herself on the floor and crossed her arms. She closed her eyes and took a big breath in. "All right. I've been out late, yes. I have been doing ballet, yes."

Zee sat next to her. "Why so late though? The Festival isn't for another month or two and we just started working within our concentrations for school."

Jameela looked down at her hands. "I'm not sure you know what it's like to be considered beautiful, particularly as a dancer, then considered problematic simply because you're maturing like every other teenage girl."

Zee's face softened. She was surprised that cool and collected Jameela finally started to open up. "Well, it was no picnic when I was cute as a baby but then went through an ugly duck phase in third grade, which my older brother, Adam, loves to revisit during every Sunday family dinner," Zee recounted.

"The ridicule for going through what every other young woman is going through is ten times worse," Jameela said. "Feeling like all of a sudden you can't move like you used to. Your leg doesn't soar as high and as bendy as it seemed to. Your teacher reminding you that you were a junior champion ballet dancer. That you moved like a Disney princess and now you move like a troll. The harder I work, the less I look like I did before. And let's not even get into what happens to your feet in ballet."

Zee thought back to Tom's comment. "What happens?"

Jameela looked at Zee. "Those stupid pointe shoes wreak havoc on your feet! My big toe is now the same size as my pinky toe!"

"But don't all ballet dancers have rough feet?"

"Oh, of course. It's pretty standard for dancers in pointe shoes to have blistered and bloodied feet. I've accepted that, no problem. It's why you won't see me in sandals at the beach as long as I'm dancing. But it still doesn't make my overall body issues any better."

"Well, it's impossible to look like what you did when you were ten," Zee said. "No one does!"

"The best ballerinas do. The top dancers essentially look like they're ten until their mid-twenties. That's how they get into top companies. That's how they become top professionals. And that's what I'm aiming to do. Or at least to use ballet to get a scholarship."

"But you don't need to rely on scholarships," Zee replied. "You're a straight-A student, and both of your parents have great jobs. You did mini engineer camp already last summer. What do you have to worry about?"

Jameela turned to Zee. "My parents think that I'm going to be an engineer or doctor, just like them. I don't want that. I don't have to just do what they do, or their parents or their neighbors do. I have passions and creativity."

Jameela stood up and walked to her dresser, looking at herself in her mirror. "When I dance, I feel alive. I feel awake. When I'm studying science or maths, I feel like I'm a robot just learning how to do programs."

Speaking of school, Zee looked down at her watch. "Oh gosh, we only have twenty minutes before classes, and I'm famished."

"I have to change clothes," Jameela said. "You can go ahead without me. I'm probably going to grab an apple and run straight to class." She plucked the bobby pins from her hair to loosen her ballerina bun, and her long, black mane cascaded down her back. Then she disappeared out of the room with some clothes and her toiletry kit in hand, a signal to Zee not to wait for her to return.

. . .

The cafeteria looked near empty at 7:59 a.m. After being picked over by hungry students, the food stations were out of food and the staffers now shuffled dirty dishes back to the kitchen for washing. Zee breezed through to grab a banana and a bagel before heading to algebra class. Tom saw her as he meandered from his table at the back of the cafeteria, having eaten alone after Jasper had to leave early to get to class. Tom's morning was free after his first class was canceled because the teacher was ill. During his alone time, he wrote a few lines down on a poem he'd been working on for his modern poetry class that afternoon.

As Tom walked toward the exit, a dark-haired girl wearing sunglasses dashed in through the entrance, hoping to grab a bite before her first class. But the cafeteria staff was no longer manning the cashier stations, so she couldn't grab—or pay for—anything and check out. Once he saw that trademark exasperated gasp, he knew exactly who she was.

Jameela leaned against the door of the cafeteria and looked down at her watch, debating whether she should go to class without a bite to eat since the night before, or if she should wait for a cafeteria staffer to help her.

Feeling sorry for the hungry classmate, Tom slowly walked up to her. He had an extra banana and a to-go cup of steel-cut oats in his bag that he was going to take back to his room for later, but he was feeling too full from his earlier serving of organic eggs, berries, and whole-wheat toast.

"Hey," he said, grabbing Jameela's attention, and offered her the oatmeal and banana. "Want some breakfast?"

Jameela looked at him, stunned. "Are you not hungry?"

"I came, I ate, and now I'm out. You look hungry. And late for class. So enjoy."

Jameela watched as Tom walked outside to the quad, peacefully striding toward the main library. She felt embarrassed that Tom had to give her a handout and worried about being late for class. She felt alone in the cafeteria and alone in her problems with ballet. But looking down at that banana as her stomach gurgled, she was sure happy to have run into Tom when she did. At least she wouldn't die of hunger in class, thanks to him.

Jameela quickly headed for the exit and called out toward the quad, "Thank you!"

Tom turned around, looked at Jameela's lithe frame and dark hair blowing in the gentle autumn air, and smiled.

16

IS ANYONE THERE?

$\mathcal{Z}$ ee sat at her desk during music theory, her mind half focused on the lecture, the other half thinking about Jameela before drifting to Izzy and Jasper. Zee was supposed to meet them for study group today. *Will it be another video shoot, or some actual study time?* she wondered.

Archie sauntered into class, two minutes late as usual, and gave a brush past Zee as he took his seat behind her. He wrote a few lines of feeble notes on the day's lesson. Then he leaned forward in his seat and turned his head.

"So, what's your plan after dinner?" Archie whispered out of the corner of his mouth toward Zee.

Zee leaned in. "I hadn't thought that far ahead."

"I've got some things I want you to hear."

Zee's eyes darted around, then settled back on Archie. "After dinner, I'll be in my dorm, since that's usually when dorm advisors come around locking the doors for check-in," Zee said.

"Ah, you and the silly rules again," Archie said, tossing his head back. "Okay then, meet me in the basement of the dining hall right after dinner. The acoustics down there are surprisingly solid. We'll jam for a bit, and then head home for your precious curfew. All right?"

Zee blinked her eyes and sighed. "Fine."

Archie slowly leaned back into his chair again. Zee slinked back in her seat, biting her lower lip, fighting the urge to blush with excitement.

· · ·

The sound of clanking plates and glasses echoed throughout the main dining hall. Students packed the tables and chatted excitedly about their days in between bites. Jasper arrived early in hopes to catch Zee before Tom and Jameela arrived. He had an extra copy of his circuitry notes and wanted to give them to Zee to help her ace the next quiz.

As Jasper put his backpack down at their regular table, Tom gave Jasper a nod from across the room as he walked toward the food station serving the day's special: salmon fishcakes and baked scotch eggs with root vegetables from the school garden. Tom instead opted for a Beyond Meat burger with no bun and some fruit, and headed toward the cashier.

Zee arrived flustered, as if she just walked in from a windstorm. "Is Jameela here?" she blurted. "I haven't seen her all day. I'm so worried about her. Did she quit school?"

"I saw her this morning," Tom said. "She was fine. Famished, but fine."

Zee took a breath, then headed for the food stations to grab a vegetarian wrap with avocado and peppers. She quickly returned to her usual seat. Jasper sat down after her with a hot bowl of soup and a roll as Tom took a bite of his burger.

As Zee unwrapped her sandwich, Jameela quietly joined them. All three paused mid-bite and looked at her.

"I'm fine, guys," Jameela said. "I don't know what theatrics Zee might have told you, but I'm fine."

"Did you make it to class?" Zee asked.

"Yes, mummy," Jameela said. "All of them, no problem." Jameela tucked into her salad, then turned toward Tom. "Thanks for the scrummy oatmeal this morning."

They went back to eating their meals, each one waiting for the other to speak next. Finally, a voice broke the silence.

"How goes it, Cali?" Archie said, sneaking behind Zee and putting his hand on her shoulder. Tom and Jameela looked up quickly, then focused on their dinners. Jasper watched them, curious what Archie wanted with Zee. "Don't forget about tonight."

"Um, right, tonight," Zee's said, stumbling over her words. Archie walked away before Zee could confirm her attendance.

Jasper's eyebrows furrowed together. He looked at Zee. "What was that?"

Zee looked down at her avocado wrap. "Oh, we're just... studying together for music class."

"You study together? Like, regularly?"

Zee looked up at Jasper. "We have one class together and he's also working on his Festival presentation. He trusts my ear, so we work together on music stuff."

"Uh-huh," Jasper said, backing away from Zee, annoyed about her making friends with the only frenemy he had in this entire school. "Well, you reckon you have time to study with me and Izzy for circuitry?"

"Of course. I was the one who invited *you* to study with *us*," Zee said. "But you guys haven't been that focused in our study groups, so who knows?"

Jasper reached for papers inside his notebook and handed them to Zee. "I'm super focused. Look, I even brought you some extra notes to help you with the next quiz."

"Oh. Thanks," she said, standing to pack up her things and head out. "I appreciate that."

"Where are you going?"

"To meet Archie. To study."

"Right now?"

"When did you think we were studying?"

"I just... I mean, I guess I assumed you were meeting at study hall."

"No, we're meeting before curfew."

Jameela looked up from her dinner. "Don't be late, dear. Should I text you twenty times if you don't make it home in thirty minutes?" The sarcasm was palpable.

"I was just concerned about you!"

"I know, Zee." Jameela waved. "See you later."

Zee grabbed her tray and her backpack. "Thanks again for the notes, Jas. I'll see you tomorrow in class."

"Yeah, don't stay out too late with your mate," Jasper snipped.

Zee was taken aback by Jasper's tone. "What does that mean? Archie and I only work on music together."

"Okay, right. Never mind."

"What does that mean?" Zee asked again.

"Nothing," Jasper said. He looked down at his tray. Zee whipped her head around and walked off. Jasper watched her leave, tapping his finger on the table, wishing Archie would find another musical partner.

• • •

Zee trotted down the stairs near the back of the dining hall toward the dimly lit basement, where there were several offices for the cafeteria and garden managerial staff and old photo displays of basketball teams, music clubs, and other organized student activities. A few of the offices were vacant and used as multipurpose rooms for student gatherings. Zee walked past one of those empty rooms and heard a few chords from an acoustic guitar.

"Cali, over here," Archie called from inside. He strummed his guitar, searching for the right chord. Zee walked toward him softly, careful not to break his concentration. Archie hummed as he looked out ahead of him.

"Are you working on a new song or the same song as before?" asked Zee.

"Dunno," Archie said. Zee noticed his foot tapped the floor every eight counts or so. Archie looked at her. "You're always so happy."

"Must be all that California sun," Zee replied as she sat down. "Do you want to play me what you've been working on?"

Archie strummed his guitar again, looking beyond Zee.

Am I invisible to you?
But my pain is invisible to none
Can't make up love with your fancy things
The damage is already done

Zee's mouth slowly relaxed into a flat horizontal position as she listened. She suddenly felt sad, like she had just gone through a breakup. *Did Archie have his heart broken by someone?* she wondered. It had to be the only explanation for why his song lyrics were so weepy.

Zee looked at Archie, her head turned downwards. "Another sad love song?" she asked.

"Rather, a lack of love song," he replied.

Zee's face looked sad as she took a step toward the seat next to him and sat down. "What's wrong?" Archie asked. "You seem down."

"No, it's just..." Zee searched for the right words. "So, you keep asking me to listen to your music as a source of inspiration, but then you keep coming up with these sad love songs. Do I make you sad?"

"No, Cali! You do the exact opposite."

"Then where is this sad inspiration coming from?" Zee asked.

Archie looked ahead at the wall ahead of him. He put his guitar to the side. "You like The Hollows, Cali?"

"Yeah, so far."

"Right. It's a great school. You been home yet?"

"No, but I was at Izzy's last weekend."

"Ah, Izzy Matthews. Quite posh, that Izzy. But your home, your parents. They're good, yeah?"

"Yeah."

"You talk to them every day?"

"Not every day, but pretty often. My mom is always in my DMs, but that's because she wants me to like her posts to boost her 'engagement.'"

"At least your mum engages," Archie said.

"What does that mean?" Zee asked.

Archie grabbed his leather jacket and started packing up his guitar. "Oy! I haven't asked you what you're working on for the Festival."

Zee hadn't quite started on anything lately. The most writing she'd done was putting her thoughts on paper for the Zee Files for Chloe and Ally. "Um, I'm not quite sure."

"Well, I'm here to offer myself as inspiration," Archie said, leaning in toward her as he grabbed his guitar and jacket. He spoke close to her face and then landed a quick kiss on her freckled left cheek. "Let me know when you're ready to jam again."

Archie walked out of the room, leaving Zee behind. Her face was as warm as the fluorescent lights shining down on her. She raised her hand to her cheek, smiled, and hurried to gather her belongings so she could make it home before curfew.

• • •

Zee made a left out of the small office space and hustled up the stairs, climbing them two at a time. At the top, the door was closed, locked from the other side. She grabbed one of the door handles and rattled it loudly. Then she banged on the window. Both were locked.

Was the entire building locked? Zee wondered. It was only 7:15 p.m. Curfew was in fifteen minutes. Did Archie make it out? Or worse—did Archie lock her in?

Zee breathed faster. *What if I'm stuck here overnight?* she thought. *What if I have to sleep here? If I can't get a comfortable night's sleep at Izzy's, how would I sleep on the cafeteria floor? Is there even a bathroom down here? And if there's no bathroom, how can I brush my teeth? And then how can I go to class with horrible morning breath? There were onions in that avocado wrap! Archie will never speak to me again. Neither will Izzy. Or Jameela. I'll be alone on campus. Stinky and alone!*

"Hello?!" Zee yelled through the door. "Stupid Archie," she mumbled under her breath.

Zee turned around and leaned her back up against the door, frustrated. *Could this be karma for hanging out with Archie instead of Jasper? Maybe Jasper ratted me out to the staff and they decided to lock me in to show me a lesson,* Zee thought. *Nah, Jasper would never do that. But did karma do this instead? Could karma could explain my poor marks in circuitry too?*

Zee held her phone tight. She started to feel claustrophobic. She looked at her watch—it was almost 7:30 p.m. The dorm advisor would come around shortly. If she missed curfew, the advisor would call her parents. And the advisor might tell her parents about her below-average grades. "Oh. My. God. I've got to get out of here."

Finally, Zee heard a rattling on the other side of the door. The door opened, and Zee spilled out to the other side. A maintenance worker stood next to Zee with a long key that looked like it unlocked a haunted house. "Sorry," the man said. "I guess we assumed everyone had left for the day down here."

"Oh thank goodness," Zee told the school employee. "Thank you for rescuing me!"

"Why were down here in the first place?"

"Impromptu jam session," she said. "Next time we'll start earlier."

Zee quickly walked to the exit of the dining hall, and once she got outside, she picked up the pace to a jog across the main quad and back to her dorm. She panted as she pumped her arms. The night air was crisp and quiet. Lights were on in most of the dorms and dim throughout the campus lecture halls and labs. Somehow, thanks to karma or the wind at her back helping her gain speed as she sprinted across the quad, Zee arrived at her dorm's entrance sweaty but with one minute until curfew to spare.

Flustered, Zee walked into her room and found Jameela sitting on the edge of her bed in leggings and an oversized nightshirt. "Dorm advisor asked about you. I told her you were working on your Festival project," she said and winked.

• • •

Zee, Jasper, and Izzy sat in circuitry class, awaiting Mr. Roth to hand out the latest quiz on last week's lesson. At her desk, Izzy flipped a pen from her pinky finger to her pointer finger. Jasper sat up tall, looking over his notes one last time before tucking his notebook underneath his desk. Zee, however, was sweating and gazing at the two of them, slightly resentful about them derailing the study sessions she'd had with them so far.

The quiz was only five questions, and Zee was confident in her answers to most of them. She handed it back to Mr. Roth, crossed her fingers and hoped for the best. Afterward, he made an announcement.

"As mentioned, the science topics change every few weeks. Next subject, we're going to study the oceans."

"Yes!" Zee said, pumping her fist. Finally, a subject she could get behind. She had done a ton of research on oceans back in Brookdale, even heading a Save the Oceans program that involved a cleanup day at a local beach. She looked over at Jasper, hoping he was just as excited. But somehow he'd ducked out of class right after he turned in his quiz, missing the announcement.

• • •

Before getting into bed, Zee checked the messages in the Zee Files. She was eager to update the girls on her basement lockout drama with Archie and her ocean study coming up in science class. In the file, she found a message from Chloe waiting for her.

Hi hi! Did you kiss Archie yet hahah? Seriously, you two could be like a musical duo for how close you're getting. Anyway, I still can't believe the news about Ally. Her parents' splitting up must really be hard for her.

Zee's eyes widened when she read the words "splitting up." As in divorce? As in no longer together?

Zee picked up the phone and texted Chloe.

Zee

I'm in the file... What about Ally's parents?

Chloe

You didn't know?

Zee

No! She didn't tell me! How could she not tell me? How do you know?

Chloe

> She texted me last weekend about it. Said she couldn't sleep and didn't want to leave it in the file. We chatted for about an hour.

Zee

> I was away at Izzy's house last weekend.

Chloe

> I know. Anyway, yes, her parents have broken up. Ally's been living with her dad for a few months. Her mom is in California for now.

A horrible feeling sank in her stomach. Ally never mentioned there was anything troubling going on at home, or that she hadn't seen her mother in months. Zee looked at her phone and realized she hadn't gotten a text from Ally in a week. While Zee was adjusting to her new school, new life, new friends, Ally had slowly slipped away, adrift in the drama of her own life.

17

GUESS WHO'S COMING HOME?

*Z*ee texted Ally via WhatsApp, but got no response. She
tried Instagram, Messenger, Squad, Quallmi, all of
the usual channels. Nothing. Then, she dialed Ally's number.
The call went straight to voicemail. Zee looked in the Zee Files
for any past messages from Ally to the group that might've
hinted about her parents splitting up. Nothing.

Zee flopped onto her bed. Her chest felt heavy. She
anxiously chewed the inside of her mouth. *How could my best
friend not tell me her parents were splitting? If my parents were
splitting, Ally would be my first call,* she thought.

Zee slumped back in her chair, rubbing her temples, trying
to massage out the stress. She reached for her journal in her
bookbag, took out a piece of paper and her favorite pen, and
started writing out her feelings, hoping the stress would emit
through her fingers and out of her head. Her breathing sped
up as her hand scrawled across the paper, filling in the lines
as her emotions spilled onto the paper:

Waiting, wondering, fading from your eye
Never knew that you were hurting
Now I know you know I know
So why are you punishing me?
All I know is what I see...

A chime dinged when her cell phone registered an incoming message. Zee scrambled for it, hoping for Ally on the other end. Instead, there was a notification from Archie.

Archie

> **What's up, Cali?**

Zee

> **Hi.**

Archie

> **I haven't heard much from you.
> Fancy a jam session this week?**

Zee looked down at her notebook and thought perhaps Archie could provide a guitar riff for the lyrics she just wrote.

Zee

> **Sure. Try to not lock me in
> the dining hall basement
> this time?**

> I still don't understand how that happened. Meet me right after class in the concert hall. We'll book a room.

Zee tossed the phone down and continued writing until her hand cramped up, her head felt clearer, and all of the lines on the page were filled with words.

• • •

Zee filed out of music theory class last, half nervous to share her writing with Archie for the first time, and half dreading spending more time with him instead of studying with Izzy and Jasper. She knew Jasper would be upset with her again. But for now, she trusted Archie would have some ideas for music to match the lyrics she was working on.

Archie was waiting outside the classroom door. "You ready?"

"Where's your guitar?"

"Stored it in the room before class so I didn't have to drag it 'round. You got something good for me?"

"Maybe," Zee said. "You still working on your song?"

"Today it's about you, Cali."

They went to practice room B, one of the smaller private rooms. Archie opened a locker toward the back of the room and took out his guitar.

"All right, Cali. You sing, I'll play."

Zee sheepishly took her notebook out of her backpack and

sat on one of the stools at the front of the room. Archie sat across from her, tuning his guitar. Then Zee cleared her throat and started to sing. She kept her eyes closed through the first verse and chorus. When she finished, she slowly peeled her eyes open again. Archie gazed at her.

"Well?" Zee asked.

Archie started to drum a chord that matched the verse perfectly. Zee sang along again: "*Waiting, wondering, fading from your eye.*" Archie changed the chord for the second line, and composed several chords in a row that matched Zee's lyrics perfectly. He stared straight ahead at her the entire time he played. When they finished, there was a moment of silence.

"That was amazing," Zee said, breathless. "I mean, I'm still working on the lyrics, but, like, this was an amazing start for the music. Wow."

Archie put the guitar to the side. "So now you're writing the sad songs," Archie said. "A surprise coming from sunny California."

Zee looked down at her notebook. A lump swelled in her throat. "Cali girls have problems too."

"Everybody's got their something," Archie said. "I haven't spoken to my mum and dad for three weeks."

Zee looked up, surprised. "Why?"

Archie shrugged his shoulders. "They're in Switzerland, I'm here. They're busy. I'm busy. Life's busy."

Zee looked down, her lower lip poking forward as she thought about Ally and Jasper both distancing themselves, her roommate's ballet issues and her moody behavior, and her less-than-stellar grades. Her temples started to throb again.

Archie grabbed his guitar and stood up. "Speaking of busy, I'm off to sport. Rugby day." He walked toward Zee and placed his hand on hers resting on her knee. "Ah, Cali, cheer up. The song's great. I'll write down these chords so you have them. And whatever's bothering you, remember, no one stays sad forever."

Zee looked up at him, locking her blue eyes with his green ones. She smiled, feeling reassured by his words. An act of kindness from Archie is an event no one on campus would expect. But Zee just lived it. And a passerby walking past practice room B witnessed it too.

That witness, however, was the last person Zee wanted to see: Jasper.

• • •

After three weeks at school, students were getting ready for fall break, a chance to go home for the week to recharge and see their families for the first time this term. Between schoolwork and drama with her friends, Zee couldn't be more ready for the rest.

Friday morning, Zee's bags were packed with her favorite sweatpants, jumpsuits, and T-shirts that she wore for her days outside the classroom. She was excited to go home and snuggle her twin siblings, to eat her mother's yummy home cooking and grill her dad about English literature so she could ace her next paper.

I'll be there at four to pick you up, Mr. Carmichael texted Zee the night before.

Awesome. Can you bring some of those sticky bun things Mom made for her Instagram feed? I'll be starving!

Friday was the last day Zee, Izzy, and Jasper would see each other, since Zee would leave Friday after school.

Zee ate a light breakfast with a cup of tea before heading to algebra class, where she sat a few rows over from Izzy. Izzy took thorough notes and kept her head in her textbook during the entire class, not once looking over at Zee. *I guess I should be doing the same,* Zee thought.

Science class was a short walk away, and usually Zee dragged her feet as she slinked toward the classroom. But today she had a light spring in her step knowing that she only had two more days of circuitry study left. Zee took her seat near Jasper, who also kept his gaze straight ahead.

At the end of class, Mr. Roth came around with their last quiz from a few days ago, the day after Jasper lent her his notes. He gently placed the exam on the corner of her desk and nodded. "Better," the teacher mumbled. Zee grabbed the paper and turned it over. A red "89" was written on the corner. Zee exhaled, and waved over to Jasper to say thank you. But he was already gone.

. . .

Zee's plan was to come back from her last class, clean up, leave her dirty clothing for laundry pickup, and head out with her bags to the main gate where students heading home for the weekend gathered to check out with the headmaster's staff.

During morning break, Mrs. Carmichael sent a text to Zee.

Mom

> Darling, your father got roped into a meeting this afternoon and won't be able pick you up. I'll see you after school, mmkay?

Zee

> Okay, and don't forget that sticky bun thing you made for your IG feed!

Zee stood outside of the main gate with the rest of her schoolmates, waiting for their parents to arrive. Izzy walked up after her, carrying a weekend bag on one shoulder. She reached the gate just as her dad drove up at 3:45 p.m. sharp in his black Range Rover, and Izzy gave Zee a quick one-armed hug and a kiss on Zee's cheek before she hopped in the front passenger seat and rode off. Zee looked around for Jasper but didn't see him. She wondered how she'd missed talking to him the entire day.

"Want me to bring you anything back from my favorite tea shop?" Tom asked as he walked near the headmaster staff's table. His Uber was waiting for him in the lot, his mother walking toward the gate.

"Hmm, some matcha?" Zee asked.

"I gotchu," he said.

"Where's Jasper? Is he not going home?"

"Think he's leaving later today. Said something about needing to finish up a sound project first. He's in the room hovering over his laptop with his headphones on. Been like that for hours."

Zee nodded slowly as Tom waved and left.

Jameela planned to stay on campus and dedicate more time to ballet practice before heading home the next day. Archie was MIA—and had been MIA since their jam session in the concert hall.

Zee looked around for her mother but didn't see her. It was five past four. She looked at her phone and was about to text her when suddenly a text came in from her mother.

Mom

> Darling, I got caught on a project and Camilla is here watching the twins while I work. I've sent an Uber for you that will arrive at four. That information is below. So sorry, darling, but I'll see you when you get home.

Who's Camilla? Zee wondered. She hadn't heard that name before. A screenshot of the Uber app with the driver's name and location came through next. Zee's heart fell as she watched parents line up at the gate and greet their sons and daughters, excited to have them back in their own home. *Was everything in my parents' lives all of a sudden more important than me?* Zee thought.

The Uber driver whose photo was in the screenshot arrived at the front gate. The headmaster nodded and waved Zee over. The driver shook Zee's hand, ushered her in the car, placed her bag in the trunk, and took off. It looked like Zee would have to wait yet a little while longer to taste those sticky buns her mother made.

Zee took out her phone and sent a message to both Chloe and Ally on her way home. Zee still wanted to reach Ally, guilty that she had to hear the news about her parents thirdhand. Zee also posted a few photos—including one of her solid B+ circuitry exam—and messages to the Zee Files. She thought to text Jasper, but instead Zee opened up Instagram and for fun went to her mom's feed. There, a new post included a photo of her mom in the kitchen smiling with the twins in the background, those sticky buns stacked neatly in a pyramid shape on a beautiful mint-green serving tray. Zee scrolled through her mom's feed and was happy she was happy, but wait, were those interlocking Cs on those sandals? *Goodness, Mom!* Zee thought. *Like she couldn't find some cool vintage slippers, or better yet, go barefoot! Cheaper, and a great excuse for a cute pedicure.*

Zee scrolled to the second photo in the third row. *Who is that smiling next to my mom?* A younger, happy dark-haired woman stood next to her mother, holding Phoebe in the backyard. They smiled at each other. The woman had on one of Mrs. Carmichael's favorite cardigans, the soft black cashmere one that Zee begged to take to school but her mom wouldn't part with. *She's not that much older than I am,* Zee thought. *Could this girl be... my replacement?*

18

NEW MEMBER OF THE FAMILY

"Hello?" Zee called out as she reached the front gate, which had a combination smart lock for which she couldn't remember the correct order of numbers. Mrs. Carmichael, dressed in a neon-pink shirtdress and fluffy mules, shuffled to the door.

"Ah! I forgot you may not have remembered the combination. Sorry, Zee. I was in the middle of a photo shoot that ran late. But I'm so happy to have you back."

"Yeah, thanks," Zee said. Mrs. Carmichael had on a thick layer of makeup, and her curly hair had been blown out straight and sleek, framing her rosy-colored high cheekbones, reminding Zee of those television news anchors back at home. The two walked through the gate, Zee dragging the suitcase behind her and up the stairs. The small batch of grass in the front yard was now framed with herbs planted along the perimeter.

The two walked through the front of the house, which included more new items since Zee had left for school. The foyer had a new bench where guests could sit to take off their shoes and place them across from the closet. In the den, a new tufted sofa, a large wood desk, and a modern chair sat across from the fireplace. Photos of the family and various California memories were also hung around the house. It felt like their old home in California, but less beachy.

Zee followed her mother to the kitchen. Phoebe and Connor, dressed in matching pajamas and vinyl bibs, squealed as they finished their snacks. She expected the twins to come waddling over to her, but instead their attention was focused on a new, older sibling-type friend feeding them baby crackers and giggling at their funny baby babble.

"Oh, Zee I want you to meet our new nanny, Camilla."

Zee blinked her eyes. This is the first she'd heard that her mother had hired a nanny.

"I've heard so much about you. So lovely to finally meet you," Camilla said politely. She turned to face the twins. "Guys, look who's here."

"Nice to meet you too," Zee said, not sure what to make of the stranger. Her face lit up when she saw her adorable young siblings as Camilla moved across the kitchen toward the stovetop. Zee planted sloppy kisses on both of their chubby cheeks. "So, do you come every day?" she asked Camilla.

"Yes, every day," Camilla said, looking at Mrs. Carmichael.

"Where's Dad?" Zee asked her mother.

"He's on his way. His meeting just finished a few minutes ago. Are you hungry, darling?"

Zee had been thinking about those sticky buns since she left campus. "Please tell me you have some of those buns left," she said.

"Of course," Camilla said, handing Zee the treat.

Camilla nuzzled Connor's neck, and Connor giggled in response. Zee knew nothing about Camilla, but Camilla seemed quite familiar in the house and with her siblings.

"How long have you been working here?" Zee asked as she bit into the bun. She closed her eyes. Yum!

"Since right after you left for school, I reckon. Your mum sent an inquiry to my agency that she was looking for a full-time live-in nanny while she worked. We got on well and I've been here ever since."

"Here? As in working here?"

Mrs. Carmichael perked up. "As in living and working here, Zee. Which has been a great help for all of us."

"If you need anything, let me know. Do you want help with your bags?" Camilla asked.

"I'm good," Zee said, watching the twins smiling up at Camilla as she moved about. *This woman from—where was she from?—is living with us? All the time? Like, she showers here?*

"Camilla is also brilliant in the kitchen," Mrs. Carmichael added. "She made the roast Cornish hens for tonight's dinner and they are delicious!"

"Right," Zee said. "I'm going to unpack and change clothes."

Zee walked up the stairs, dragging her suitcase behind her, and turned the corner toward her room. Mrs. Carmichael shuffled behind her. "Oh darling, I moved your bed to the spare bedroom like you wanted."

"Okay. But this is still my bedroom."

"Well, I thought since you love your bed so much that we'd move your bedroom to the one down the hall. Camilla sleeps here now."

Zee stood still. *Camilla has been a caregiver for barely a month and now she sleeps in my room?* "So you moved me to the guest bedroom? I'm a guest in my own house?"

"No, darling, I moved you with your bed. Which is now in the guest bedroom. So the guest bedroom is now your room, and your old room is now Camilla's room."

Zee rolled the bag toward the guest room—*her* room—and found her bed was set up facing the window, which looked at the back of the house. The blue bean bag she had placed under the window of her own room was haphazardly tossed in a corner, though her books, dresser, and mirror had been thoughtfully arranged. Instead of the colorful walls she had in her California home, her mother painted the walls a neutral gray and installed sconces beside the bed. The sunset wasn't visible from the window.

"A guest in my own house," Zee mumbled.

Camilla trailed behind her. "Is there anything I can help you with? You should have towels already laid out in your room. And I made sure to restock your shampoo and conditioner in the shower. And your favorite body lotion."

"Um, thanks." *She cooks, she cleans, she takes care of the twins and stocks my bathroom. Those were all the things Mom used to do, Zee thought. Maybe Zee wasn't being replaced after all. But maybe her mother was.*

As Zee unzipped her suitcase, fishing for her favorite leggings and jumper, her phone buzzed. On the screen was a highly anticipated notification from Ally.

Ally

> Got your messages. Sorry, was in the middle of an awkward family dinner.

Zee texted her back immediately:

Zee

> So is it true about your parents?

Ally

> Yes.

Can we talk?

Like a conference call?

No, friend to friend. I want to talk to you.

There was a long pause before Zee saw Ally typing again. *Now you want to talk?* Ally wrote. *You haven't been around the past few weeks, practically call my writing garbage while I'm going through a tough time at home, then you miss our calls with Chloe.*

I was away last weekend, and I've only missed one call, Zee defended. *And I made minimal edits on your paper. But sorry, I've only been moving to a new country and a new school and a new home the past few weeks.*

Ally didn't respond right away.

Zee typed into the phone. *I'm home for fall break now and I have time to chat without any distractions. I could even come to see you in Paris if you wanted.*

No need, I won't be here this week. Zee could feel the bitterness from Ally in each message. Yet again, Ally blew off the chance to see Zee in person.

I'm sorry to hear about your parents, Zee offered. *If my parents split, I don't know what I'd do.*

You'd split your time between one emotionally detached parent and one emotionally tortured one, wondering why they can't just get along and why your mother keeps buying you clothes and bags and things every time she sees you as if you're a charity case while your father just throws himself into work so he doesn't have to deal with you. Ally wrote in one long text message.

Zee was stunned. Ally always appeared so poised in her photos. Her essay about being an American girl in Paris sounded so dreamy. Yet somehow she felt invisible. Like a burden on her parents.

Ally, I'm so sorry. You seemed so happy in Paris. I assumed all was well.

Picking up a phone would help.

Zee's eyes froze ahead of her. She brought her fingers to the side of her head. The throbbing by her temples had returned.

Zee took out her notebook of lyrics and reviewed the song she wrote last week. She scribbled more words as they popped into her head—leaving, abandon, confession, heartache. Misunderstanding.

"Misunderstanding," she read aloud.

She let those words linger, thinking about how they made her feel, how they made the people around her feel. She misunderstood Ally, assumed her friend was living this perfect Parisian life based on that essay and her always being out and about, but the truth was her home life was in shambles. Zee misunderstood Jameela, thinking she was perfect and polished at everything she did. It turned out she was struggling with her ballet and her body image. Even Archie was misunderstood— people assumed he was this loner bad boy at school, but he was writing emo lyrics about his abandoned homelife. Like he had said, everyone's got their something.

• • •

Zee sat on her bed in the guest bedroom, feeling heavy. Her body melted into the comforter, her mind on overdrive from squabbling with Ally. She thought back to a few lunch conversations with Tom about meditation. "It's simple," he had said. "Eyes closed, body relaxed, breathe deeply and evenly." Zee laid back now with her eyes closed, breathing heavily into her chest, letting the air travel up her nostrils and into her lungs. She thought about Tom and his super chill vibe and wondered what he would do to relieve stress. She tried to breathe away all of her worries: grades, classes, Ally. Archie. Jasper. Everything. Inhale in, exhale out. Her pulse slowed.

She thought about what had happened over the past few weeks. Moving thousands of miles away from home and her friends to create a new home with new friends. Moving to a new school. Meeting new friends. A road trip to a YouTube star's country estate. A new musical partner. Crush. Friend. Something. And her old pal Jasper, whom she loved hanging out with at Brookdale, but now something felt slightly off between them. Zee's head swirled at all of the things now in her orbit, her head and heart.

"Zee, dinner's in a few minutes," Camilla called out.

Zee rose from the bed and looked around her room. *Where are the rest of my things?* Zee thought. *My mementos? My pictures? My artwork?* She walked toward what was now Camila's room and took a peek inside. The room was extremely tidy, with a four-poster bed made from brushed steel and a plush weighted comforter with several large embroidered pillows. A dresser was in one corner, a desk in another. *This was a room designed for Instagram, not me,* Zee thought.

Downstairs, Mr. Carmichael walked through the front door and gave cheery hellos to his family. The twins squealed at seeing him and jumped up and down excitedly, and Mr. Carmichael leaned down to kiss them both. Zee overheard the commotion while she was changing her clothes and getting ready for dinner. She went into the bathroom and brushed her teeth. Then she smoothed jojoba oil on her curly hair and swept her curls up into a high loose bun.

Walking back to her bedroom, Zee put on her favorite lounge pants and a jumper, then took one last look in the mirror. Her phone buzzed again. A notification from Ally.

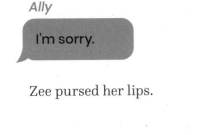

Ally

I'm sorry.

Zee pursed her lips.

Zee

Me too.

A moment passed while Ally continued typing. Zee waited anxiously for the message to send.

And yes, I owe you a tour of Paris, Ally wrote. *When can you come?*

THE END

Read on to see what happens with Zee and her friends in Book 2 of The Zee Files, *All that Glitters*.

1

FAMILY REUNION

"Zee, darling, breakfast is ready!" Mrs. Carmichael called. Mackenzie Blue Carmichael turned over in her bed on the third floor of her London home and looked toward the window, searching for her cell phone to check the time. Her hand whacked against the nightstand, knocking over her journal, but she caught her phone before it could fall to the ground too. The oversized numbers on the screen read 7:15 a.m. Zee had looked forward to sleeping in a bit longer than she would back on campus at The Hollows Creative Arts Academy, but alas, between the twins rising at sunup and her father's early schedule, the whole house had been dressed and ready for the day for the past hour.

Zee sat up in bed and looked at her phone with tired eyes. A message had come in from Ally, her BFF currently living in Paris. It was a copy of the train schedule from London to Paris for the next week.

Ally and Zee have been best friends since they both lived

in California and attended the same grade school, Brookdale Academy. Ally moved to Paris a few years ago, and Zee just moved to London at the end of summer after her father took a new job. Zee and Ally planned to meet up in Paris this week while Zee was on fall break—Ally's parents recently split up, and she could use some cheering up from her bubbly and energetic friend Zee.

Let me check and see which day will work! Zee texted back. She was excited to make this trip happen, especially since Ally had canceled on her when they scheduled their first reunion in Paris right before school started.

Zee threw back the covers, swung her legs off the edge of the bed, and sat up. She stretched her arms overhead and rose to her tippy toes before relaxing her heels back down to the floor. It was her first night's sleep back in her London home since she went off to boarding school. There was something so comforting about her old bed, the way the worn-in mattress hugged her body and the softness of her favorite flannel sheets.

Her bed at The Hollows Creative Arts Academy, the boarding school she transferred to at the beginning of the school year, was comfortable but not yet familiar. But it didn't matter—by the time her head hit the pillow at night, Zee was so exhausted from the day as a new year nine student that she could fall asleep on any flat surface.

The schoolwork was challenging. Whether it was the language differences or the teaching styles, Zee found it hard to concentrate on the lectures. She was hoping her parents wouldn't ask how her grades were. Why ruin a great week home with disappointing news?

Luckily, making new friends has been easier than making

high marks. Zee's roommate, Jameela Chopra, was a sharp and intellectual ballet dancer who showed Zee the ropes of boarding school, though she had high standards for herself and everyone else. Izzy Matthews, a popular year nine student thanks to her YouTube channel with 50,000 followers, invited Zee to her study group, then to her Cotswolds family estate for a sleepover. Zee also has her friend Jasper Chapman, who attended Brookdale Academy for a year until he returned to London this past summer. He was the only person Zee knew in London before her first day at school.

And then there was Archie Saint John. Mysterious guy on campus. Talented guitarist. Few friends, but lives a very posh life. Zee met Archie on the first day of school after she ran into him—literally—on the quad. The two had hit it off over their music interests, and Archie invited Zee to a few jam sessions to work on their performances for the Creative Arts Festival coming up near the end of fall term. He paid Zee more attention than he did to anyone else at school. Maybe they were just friends. Or maybe more? Zee has spent more hours trying to figure out what's really going on between her and Archie than she has on her studies. As of now, she has neither the grades nor a label to describe her thing with Archie to show for her time.

Knock knock knock! "Zee, honey, would you like me to make you something to eat?"

Camilla, the Carmichael family's new nanny, was waiting for a response on the other side of the door. Zee's eyes widened as she turned her head. She thought to open the door and face Camilla directly, which would be the polite thing to do. But to Zee, Camilla still felt like a stranger, even though she'd been taking care of her family members since the school year began. Zee couldn't let a stranger see her with morning breath and crazy bed head.

"Um, I'll be down in a minute. I can grab something then," Zee replied. She waited for Camilla's footsteps to fade away, then headed to the restroom, brushed her teeth, washed her face, and got dressed for the day.

• • •

The kitchen of the Carmichael family's Notting Hill residence smelled like coffee and sounded like a train station. Phoebe and Connor, Zee's twin siblings, waddled across the floor, following their mother as she looked for a serving plate. Mr. Carmichael took a few sips of coffee while checking his e-mails on his phone. "Looks like I have a meeting at 5 p.m. Might be a bit late home tonight," he warned anyone within earshot.

"Okay, darling," Mrs. Carmichael responded. She fluttered past her husband and gave him a kiss on the cheek before she breezed toward the pantry. "I've got a meetup with the girls today."

"The girls as in your daughters?" he asked.

"No, the girls as in the Mummy Mums," Mrs. Carmichael said.

"Who?" Zee asked as she walked up behind her mother. Her father looked back at his phone.

Mrs. Carmichael explained, "They're my new mom friends. I met them at a park a few weeks ago while I was out with the twins. They all live close by and have young children, and they plan playdates and outings. They're very connected too. One of them, Sophie, sat next to me on a bench and helped me get Phoebe settled when she was fussy. She was so lovely. She introduced me to her friends, and now I'm sort of part of the circle."

"You get together every day with them?" Zee asked, sitting down at the kitchen table. "And the kids too?"

"Not every day, and not always with the kids."

"I've never met these new friends, honey," Mr. Carmichael chimed in.

"Well, you will," Mrs. Carmichael responded.

Zee looked at her mom. Her mother's curly hair, usually left long and loose in California, was tied into a low bun and smoothed back with a printed silk scarf. She wore a beautifully tailored gray tea-length dress and a tall pair of boots. In California, her mother had lived in vintage T-shirts and cut-off shorts, or long, wide-legged linen pants and sneakers. She sure has adapted to her London surroundings, Zee thought.

Mrs. Carmichael grabbed a large platter from the bottom pantry shelf and handed it to Camilla, then walked to the sitting nook where Zee was enjoying her breakfast. Mrs. Carmichael leaned over the cup of coffee she was holding with two hands. "And what's on your agenda today, Zee?"

Zee looked down at the plate of eggs, perfectly browned toast and jam, and sliced fruits Camilla had artfully arranged for her. "Probably a little more of this," she responded.

"Well, darling, I was hoping we could do something fun together while you were here. You know, maybe some shopping or a nice lunch somewhere in town."

Zee looked at her mother, whose British accent had become

so much more pronounced in the few weeks Zee's been gone. "Ally texted me last night and said she does want to meet up in Paris now. Did you know her parents were splitting up?"

"No, really?" her father said. "That's a shame."

"Yeah, I think her mother is back in California," Zee said. "Anyway, can I go to Paris this week to meet up with her?"

Mr. Carmichael made his way toward the door. "I can't do it this week, Zee. I'm on a shoot for a new campaign that I have to oversee."

Mrs. Carmichael perked up. "Zee, maybe we should go together! We can leave the twins with Camilla and you and I can have a girls trip."

Zee couldn't remember the last time she hung out with her mother alone since the twins arrived. While she appreciated her mother's offer, Zee was more excited to connect with Ally about important things, like how Ally was getting along with her dad, and how Zee was getting along with school—and, most importantly, Archie.

"I haven't seen Ally in so long. We have so much to catch up on," Zee said.

"I understand," Mrs. Carmichael said. "Tell you what, I'll take you to Paris and then give you and Ally some space to hang out. I'll sit at a different table at the restaurant or something. And then we can shop and come back home. Ooh, there's that amazing macaron shop we can check out while we're there. Sound good?"

Quality time with her best friend in Paris. Mom as a socially distanced chaperone. And macarons? "I'm in!" Zee said.

Acknowledgments

First and foremost, I'd like to say a big thank you to my A-Team at Target: Christina Hennington, Ann Maranzano, and Kate Udvari. Thank you for giving new life to this beloved character and for allowing her journey to continue.

To Jennifer Newens and the entire West Margin Press family, thank you for giving *The Zee Files* a home.

To Andre Des Rochers, thank you for your counsel over the last fifteen years. This project has gotten to this point because of you. And to the entire Granderson Des Rochers team, thank you for all of your hard work and dedication to this project.

To Stephanie Smith, Veronica Miller Jamison, and Melissa Alam, thank you for bringing *The Zee Files* to life! Your writing and art has propelled this project beyond my wildest dreams.

To my little love, Phoebe, thank you for answering all my texts and making sure *The Zee Files* is as realistic as possible. Being your aunt and living through your real-life tween adventures is the highlight of my life.

To my family: Mom, Dad, Adrianne, Erica, Marcus, Lisa, and William, thank you for being here for me and supporting me. Sheldon, Willie, and Francesca, thank you for being the best bonus siblings a sister could have.

To my Supper Club: Abdallah, Andrew, Ari, Joe, Melissa, Michelle and Vidya, thanks for being my happy place, no matter what.

Michelle, your countless hours of advice and encouragement helped me stay the course. I am forever grateful, and so are my readers. I love you always.

And finally to my readers, thank you. Thank you for bringing renewed purpose to my life and my work. Thank you for loving these characters and sticking with me.